Journey to the Ice

By Jennifer Slattery

Cover Design by Cathy Davis.

Library of Congress: 2008912006

Myth Slayers Ministries
Kansas City, MO 64060

Chapter 1

Colossians 2:8 "Beware lest any man spoil you through philosophy and vain deceit, after the traditions of men, after the rudiments of the world and not after Christ."

Makir sat in the shade of a gently waving fig tree. The wind danced through his thick black hair. A curling strand rested above his dark eyes, the ends tickling his lashes. He lifted a dirtied hand and brushed the hair out of his eyes. The family goat nibbled the soft tender grass only a few feet away. Filo, the goat, was mindful today, and for that Makir was glad. Some days the goat would get an adventurous spirit and take to wandering off. Many times he had made it past the valley of the great rivers before Makir could stop him. This was not only inconvenient, but deadly as well. Wild creatures roamed the great deserts beyond Babylon's borders, ready to devour not only the goats that wandered off, but the young boys who tended them as well. To prevent attacks from wild beasts and large birds, the boys of Babylon guarded their animals in pairs. There was safety in numbers. Today Makir's father had paired him with Mikola, a boy from the Niloth family.

Mikola and Makir didn't get along. Mikola's father was a musician at the city temple and he felt this entitled him to special privileges, like the best grazing land in the valley. As if that wasn't bad enough, Mikola spent most of his time talking about how great he was. He made sure everyone was aware of his thickly woven cloaks, dyed in the most extravagant colors, those available only to the very wealthy. He talked about the strength of his bloodlines and the enormity of his family's wealth. Mikola spent so much time talking about himself that Makir could hardly bear to be in his presence.

Not wanting to deal with him today, Makir sat many lengths away. His jaw clenched as he watched the ruddy haired boy strut among the clovers, his chest puffed out so far it looked like it would burst through the brightly colored tunic he was wearing. Perhaps tomorrow his luck would change and he could work beside Lystra, his best friend. But this was unlikely. His father preferred to pair him with those holding the greatest influence, and since all the power lay with the priests, to be a musician at the temple of the gods made you a man of great importance. And great wealth. Tolah, Makir's father, hoped Makir and Mikola would become friends, opening the door for friendship between himself and Mikola's father.

Makir wished he could tend his goat on his own. He carried smooth stones and pointed sticks with him, but he knew they were no match for the great cats and giant lizards that lurked the land. An eagle with a wingspan the size of a grown man circled up ahead. Makir held his breath and readied his spear. Usually, his aim was poor and offered little in the way of defense, but seeing the other boys with spears in hand made him feel a little better. Should the eagle attack, surely one of them would hit him.

"Makir! Makir!"

Makir turned his attention towards the sound of the voice. Siseral, his oldest sister, was running towards him, her long brown hair bouncing along her slender shoulders. She held the hem of her long, tattered dress in one hand as the other hand pumped furiously beside her. Other girls followed, each running in the direction of their kin.

"Come quickly!" she gasped. Her thin eyebrows pinched together in the center of her tanned forehead. "Nimrod has returned from the great hunt. He will speak."

Makir's stomach did a flip. Did Nimrod have news? Was all well? He searched his sister's face, but it provided no answers except those she had already given. Her face bid him hurry. He immediately jumped to his feet and grabbed his goat around the middle.

Nimrod was the leader of Babylon and a powerful warrior. He had gone to the great lands of the west to hunt the wild beasts with the scaly skin. Everyone awaited his news. Makir ran as quickly as he could, anxious to hear of the mighty man's conquests.

Filo did not like being restrained and let Makir know by nipping at his arms and arching his back. Makir gripped him all the more tightly and pressed the goat to his body. It was very difficult to run with the flailing goat in his arms.

"Hurry! You must tell father!" Siseral said.

She ran a few paces behind him, her breath coming in and out in short spurts. Her dress made a soft swishing sound as her feet raced across the grass.

"I'm going as fast as I can," Makir replied.

The goat strained against his arms and jabbed a sharp hoof into his left rib. Makir winced and tightened his grasp. Makir saw Mikola's freckled face, all puffy and red, out of the corner of his eye and let out a hearty laugh. Apparently a life of ease and privilege had put him at a disadvantage when it was time to move quickly.

"I'd like to see Mikola face the great Behemoth," Makir thought. "I'm sure his bloodlines would greatly please the great dragon's stomach."

Makir stifled another laugh, threw a casting glance at Mikola and then lengthened his stride by at least half a length. Satisfied that he had sufficiently increased his position, he raced down the crowded streets towards the center of the city. Men and women surged around him, weaving in and out of people like herds of ants scurrying for falling crumbs. The noise and rush of the crowd only made Filo thrash all the more. Once again, his sharp hooves stabbed into Makir's side. Makir winced and nearly dropped him. By the time Makir made it to his den, his sides ached. He grabbed a thick piece of twine and tied the now frantic animal to a large vase filled with olive oil. This would hold him until he got back. Then he raced off towards his father's metal shop. It didn't take him long to reach it.

When he got there, he quickly scanned the room. His father stood in the far east corner of his shop, bent over a lump of clay. Wiry gray hair fell over his face like a thick clump of wool. Bakal, Haron and Ehumed, three of Makir's brothers, were at the great furnace in the back melting stones to bring out the pure copper hidden within. Thick black smoke filled the room with the scent of burning metal, stinging Makir's eyes. His brothers immediately stopped what they were doing and gave Makir their full attention. Tolah, Makir's father, looked up but remained at work.

"What is it, my son?" Tolah asked smoothly. Thick lines edged their way across his forehead.

Tolah had a calm confidence that brought Makir great

reassurance. Never had Makir seen his father lose control. Never had Tolah shown fear.

"Nimrod has returned," Makir said.

Tolah covered the clay with a damp cloth and wiped his large hands on his already muddied apron. He glanced out at the busy street. Voices rose with excitement as people hurried past, anxious to hear what Nimrod had to say.

Makir's brothers stood at the door as Tolah carefully cleaned up his shop. Bakal looked as if he was ready to explode, his hazel eyes darting from face to face like a frenzied bull, but he held his tongue in proper respect. Makir's heart raced with excitement. After what felt like an eternity, Tolah led them out of the shop and down the street. Makir wanted to run along with many of the other townsmen racing beside him, but he willed his feet to remain steady. His father walked calmly and surely, his head held high. The boys followed obediently, their leather sandals clomping along the stone-covered path. Makir fought to slow his breathing and wondered if their slow pace was as difficult for his brothers to keep as it was for him.

By the time they got to the city center, it was already crowded with people. Red, brown, blond and black heads bobbed up and down, wide eyes peering beneath the sea of color. Tolah scanned the crowd for his wife and daughters. Makir's mother, Sharai, was pressed between a large group of women, baby Mila swung over her hip. Her soft gray eyes met Tolah's. With a slight smile, she began to push her way through the noisy mob. Makir's sisters, Siseral and Esthera, were a little less bold. They gingerly wove their way through the crowd, following quite a distance behind.

Nimrod sat on a large stone chair centered on a rectangular white slab a man's height in length and width. This had been cut from a single stone. His head, covered by a shiny copper helmet shone in the sun. The helmet had been made by Tolah and bore his signature swirls and loops, each so finely detailed they looked as i they had been painted by hand. Priests and priestesses stood to each side of him in brightly dyed robes, sharpened daggers at their sides

Manasseh, the second most powerful man in Babylon and the priest of the great sun god Utuh, stepped forward. He waved a burning stick covered in jasmine oil in front of the crowd. The people dropped to their knees with their hands raised in front o them. Makir knelt as well, not wanting to cause attention to himself but he kept his eyes on Manasseh. The priest turned to the holy men and women seated beside Nimrod and waved the incense in front o them. The air was filled with a sickly sweet smell. As the incense passed in front of each priest, they pressed their palms together and raised their hands to the sky. They chanted words Makir could no understand. After each priest had been surrounded by the swee smelling smoke, Manasseh turned to Nimrod and waved the torch in front of him. Nimrod stood and raised his arms to the sky as well only his were outstretched. Now the chanting grew louder.

"Rise!" Nimrod said, motioning with his hand for the townspeople to stand.

The priests stopped their chants and everyone stood in silence.

"As you know," Nimrod said. "I have been on a journey to the west in search of the giant lizards that steal our animals and children. I have had great success!"

The crowd cheered loudly. Nimrod watched them with pleasure, his chest inflating with pride. His eyes held a wild, hungry look as if he were feeding off their frenzy. After a few moments he raised his hand again to silence them. He continued in a loud firm voice.

"This journey brought more than safety from the great scaly lizards." His dark eyes blazed. "This journey brought back to our city the favor of the gods," Nimrod said. "And now it is your turn to honor them. Three more have joined the ranks of the great immortals, and if we bring them the honor they require, I too, will become one of them. At the proper time."

At this some gasped and others began to cheer once again. A few stared in disbelief. Makir didn't know what to do. Was this a good thing?

Nimrod continued, "We will build a great temple, a temple that will reach all the way to the heavens. We will make a name for ourselves among all the other men of the earth. We will join in the work of the gods."

"Yeah! We will!" the townspeople yelled again and again. "We will make a name for ourselves! We will be great men on the earth!"

The crowd grew wilder and louder. People began to press their way forward, their arms waving in the air, fists clenched. Makir was shoved back and forth, elbows jabbing into his sides. Baby Mila began to cry and clung to her mother's neck. Makir looked to his father. His expression was cool and void, but his eyes held a slight spark.

Once again, Nimrod silenced them. "You will all serve in the building of the temple. Every male over ten will dedicate six dashes on the sundial to the gods each day. Those with many sons may increase their son's labor and use it in place of their own service. All females over ten will help with the sacrificial meals and temple decorations. Only the matriarch of the family may stay home to tend to the needs of the household."

Once again gasps were heard, only this time they were not gasps of joy but were instead, those of dread. Women began to talk among each other, worried of how this would affect the affairs of their household. What would happen to the families with many daughters but no sons? How would their family work? Who would tend the great wheat and barley fields? What would happen to the many shops in the market square? Could the city of Babylon survive such a burden?

"Silence!" Nimrod yelled.

The talking stopped instantly. Nimrod's eyes contracted sharply. His piercing glare caught Makir's eyes and held them. Makir's heart cramped within his chest, but he could not look away. He felt a chill surround him. An evil smile spread across Nimrod's face. Satisfied by Makir's reaction, he returned his attention to the crowd.

"If the temple is not done to the gods' liking, they will send another great flood, perhaps even worse than the one that destroyed the earth 200 years ago. If they do, only I and my loyal priests and priestesses will be spared. The rest of life on earth will be completely destroyed!"

Makir felt the blood drain to his feet. He had heard stories of this great flood, stories of total destruction and devastation. You could still see the evidence left behind. Large canyons had been cut in the strongest of rocks as if they were made of cheese, their centers left as layers of sand and soil scattered throughout the land. The thought of such a torrent filled him with dread.

"You...you...you," Nimrod began to call men out of the crowd. He called five men in all. These men stepped forward. "You will stay. The rest of you go, but you must report to the city center by midday tomorrow," Nimrod said.

The townspeople slowly began to head home. Makir listened to the many conversations around him.

"What am I to do? We have but one son, and he is very ill," a woman said. She had a long, sallow face set in a nest of tangled gray hair.

"And what of me? We need our sons to tend to our fields," replied the woman next to her. She looked as if she were expecting a child. Her belly was round and full and her face was flushed from the heat of the sun. Her eyes grew wet as she continued. "How will we bargain at the markets if we have no grain to bargain with?" she asked.

Many more voiced their concern, but many were excited as well.

"We will make a great name for ourselves! We shall be as the mighty gods! This is a time as never before, to have such a mighty man as Nimrod in our presence, a man who communes with the gods themselves! Perhaps we will all become gods!"

Makir's skin pricked with anxiety. For some reason, his heart would not stop racing. He felt as if he had just jumped from a high cliff and was plummeting to the ground. Why couldn't he have the peace of his father? Why did he feel such fear and dread?

Chapter 2

The rest of the day was a blur. His brothers had gone back to the family copper shop to set things in order for the coming day. They would probably have to work late into the night to make up for the time they would lose once work on the temple began.

Makir stayed home and tried to help his mother. She too had much work to do. It would be a great hardship to lose so many hours of his sisters' aid. Bread had to be made for the coming days, figs had to be gathered, stews had to be prepared. Even though their needs would be great, only so much could be done ahead. No matter how heavily you spiced the dishes, the food still quickly spoiled in the hot sun. How could Sharai manage all the food preparation on her own?

Later that afternoon, Makir sat in the center of his cool earthen home, watching his sisters run about frantically as they tried to do a week's worth of work in less than a few hours. Siseral knocked over an earthen jar, spilling an entire month's worth of oil onto the smooth dirt floor. The warm liquid seeped into the dirt before she could salvage even one drop, leaving nothing more than a large discolored oval in its place. Makir's mother groaned and made a lunge at her daughter, but Siseral darted out of the way just in time. Sharai heaved a loud sigh, spat a few hateful words at her already wounded daughter and turned back to her work. Makir watched them in sadness. His heart ached for his sister as he watched her scurry across the room, her eyes always on her mother, desperate for any sign of approval, or forgiveness. If only he could help, then perhaps his sister would not make so many mistakes. But no, this would not be proper. Besides, he was not trained in the skills of the home. His primary job was tending the goat, at least, for now.

Once he was ten, he would begin training at his father's shop. Makir could hardly wait! He especially looked forward to the day when his father would let him form his own molds from the soft clay.

Makir's mother stood over a boiling pot of lentils and onions, sweat and steam dripping from her face. She turned and looked at Makir.

"Your father and brothers will not be joining us for the evening meal," Sharai said. "Surely there is much to be done before work begins on the great temple." She grabbed a heavy clay vessel from a wooden crate beside her and filled it with bubbling red broth. "Bring this stew to them quickly before it gets cold and see if there is anything else they need," she said.

Makir jumped to his feet, glad to have an excuse to leave. He

11

loved to visit his father's shop. He loved to watch his brothers stir the hot stones until they melted into thin syrup. It always amazed him how such ordinary stones could be turned into such shiny works of art by just a little heat and time. His father had great skill and could create vases with marvelously patterned indentations less than a hair in width. This skill had been passed to him from his father and was now being passed down to Makir's brothers. In two years, when Makir turned ten, he too, would learn this skill and would then pass it on to his sons after him. The art of metalworking had been in their family for four generations now.

When Makir got to his father's shop, he was surprised at how busy it was. Impatient men and women crowded around a small earthen counter. Bakal stood on the other side of the counter, a wet slab of clay and stylus in his hand. On the clay were three columns and under each column were numerous tally marks.

Makir walked over to his other brother Ehumed. "What is going on?" he asked.

Ehumed set a large crate of stones on a shelf and wiped the sweat from his brow. "They have come for images of these new gods Nimrod spoke of. Father is making the molds for them now," Ehumed said. "One is already finished and drying. It will be ready for pouring tomorrow."

"Will Father be able to complete so many orders on his own? Will you be able to help him at all? Once your six dashes of service are through?" Makir asked. He set the already cooling pot of lentils on the counter and looked over at his father.

Tolah's hands moved quickly and surely. "We will come as soon as our work at the temple is done, but father thinks our time is best spent in service to the gods, not to him," Ehumed said. A streak of chalky grey clung to his cheek. He reached up to wipe a bead of sweat off his forehead, leaving another streak of grey just above his eyes. "He says if we honor them in this way, they will honor us, and our work. They will make our city great! And as you can see," he motioned to the group of people squeezed into the shop and lined along the street, "he is right. Already the gods have blessed our obedience."

Perhaps, with his older brothers busy at the temple and his father's work load increased, perhaps his father would allow Makir to begin his training early. It was true, 10 was the customary age for boys to learn the family business, but so much was changing now. Maybe this custom could be changed as well.

Makir held his breath and walked over to his father. In his mind, he tried to plan his words. Once his father gave him an answer, there would be no changing his mind. Somehow Makir had to convince his father that this was the proper thing to do under the current circumstances. Makir could convince him that he was older in manner than his age claimed, having so many other brothers to follow after. No, that wouldn't work. For with his father, it wasn't the age itself, but the tradition upheld by the age. His father had great respect for his own father, Tahoma, a man of strict traditions and customs.

Makir's grandfather had died from sickness many, many seasons ago. The stargazers and priests said an evil spirit had taken hold of him. They said the people of Babylon had been slow to honor the new gods Nimrod had revealed. According to them, the gods had been greatly angered by this and had caused great sickness to the elder members of the city. It was the elders' duty to see that the younger generation followed the necessary laws and customs, and they were held responsible for the disobedience of their children.

Maybe Makir could tell him that he would be serving the

gods by working in the shop. No! He could not do that. The very thought made his stomach clench and sent prickles through his skin. He didn't know why, but something about serving the gods made him feel very uneasy. What would his father say if he were to find out how irreverent Makir was? Makir pushed the thought out of his mind, unable to comprehend what it would feel like to have his father disappointed in him. Surely there was something else he could say, something to convince Tolah he was man enough to help.

Not knowing what to say, Makir just stood and stared at his father. His heart raced.

"What is it, son?" Tolah asked patiently.

"You are busy," Makir replied.

His father nodded and then returned to his work. He pressed a moist lump of clay into the counter in front of him, kneading it swiftly and forcefully with his large hands.

"If only my brothers could stay and help tomorrow," Makir said.

The minute the words were out of his mouth, he regretted it. Tolah's head snapped up. He stared into his son's eyes. For a brief minute, Makir could see emotion, either fear or anger, he was not sure which, but then Tolah's face quickly smoothed to its usual calmness. Makir stared at the clay in front of him, unable to meet his father's eyes.

"It is good that your brothers serve the gods in this way," Tolah said. "Utuh brings light to our land every morning, and Nanna brings light to our land at night. Inanna holds our families together and keeps hunters strong in our land. And now, we have three more gods to bless our land and our people."

Tolah rolled the clay into a smooth, round ball and set it on a circular stone. The round, flat stone could be turned around and around as he fashioned the lump of clay.

"You heard what the great Nimrod said. We are about to make a name for ourselves, to share in the work of the gods. He is a great leader, that man. Only he can lead ordinary men into the heavenly realms."

He turned the stone slowly, gently pulling the clay upward and outward. Makir so longed to touch the smooth clay. He knew he could make the most beautiful vases and bowls, like no one had ever made before. Someday he would have his own shop, an even grander shop than that of his father's. He could wait no longer. His father might say no, but it wouldn't do him any good to remain silent. And if Tolah were ever to say yes, now would be the most likely time.

"I think I could be of great use to you, Father," Makir said quietly, his eyes fixed on the clay in front of him.

His father didn't respond, and after a while, Makir began to wonder if perhaps he hadn't heard him.

"I think I could be of great use to you, Father, if you let me," Makir spoke quickly. "I could load the furnace with stones and skim the unwanted remains from the top of the boiling liquid. I could sweep the dust from the floor and see to it that the metal is not wasted. I learn quickly. I would like to honor you in this way."

Makir's heart beat wildly in his chest as he waited for his father's response.

Tolah stood up from his stool and wiped his hands on his apron. He looked at his son for a long time and then looked at the growing crowd of people filling his shop.

"And what of Filo?" Tolah asked.

"I would take him to the fields early before the sun is high, and again in the evening, when my work here is done. The rest of the day I would tie him to the olive oil vase or in a shaded area of the market square. Many of us goat tenders will work together, taking turns watching over the goats." Makir's words spilled out quickly.

"I will talk with your mother," Tolah replied.

Tolah sat back down and began to turn the stone again. Makir wanted to jump up and down and yell for joy, but he forced himself to remain composed. He had to show his father he was a man, capable of great responsibilities. Oh, how he hoped his mother would say yes! Wanting to gain as much favor as he could, he decided to go home and see if his mother needed any help.

Lystra was waiting at his house when he got there.

"I heard your father has become a man of great demand," Lystra said. "I should feel privileged to be your friend. Can your highness spare some time to toss a few stones?"

Makir had intended to help his mother, but he didn't want to look like a fool in front of his best friend, especially after the 'your highness' jokes. Still, he really wanted to be allowed to help his father, and he knew if his mother were pleased with him, there was a better chance of that. His father may be the head of the home, but his mother was the head of his father's heart.

"I can't. My mother needs me," he said.

"Sure, your majesty!" Lystra sneered. "I know it must be hard being such a valued member of society. I would hate to see you waste any of your precious time on a cloth dyer's son such as myself." Lystra laughed and walked away.

Even though Lystra had been joking, the words cut deep into Makir's heart. He so needed Lystra's friendship. A lump formed in his throat as he thought about the few friends he truly did have. In fact, Lystra was his only one, and even this friendship was shaky. Bakal said he was too sensitive. Too weak. But then, Bakal thought every man weak who chose his mind over his fists. Yet this was the way of Babylon. It was the men with the greatest strength who held the greatest honor. Even the holy men and wise men were chosen for their great hunting skill. Each one of them had served with Nimrod loyally before the gods had chosen them for service in the temple.

Makir walked into the cool, dark den that was his home. It took a moment for his eyes to adjust to the darkness. His mother was pressing olives between two stone slabs. The slabs had small slits cut into them. This allowed the oil to drain and pool while keeping the pulpy flesh on the surface.

"You do not wish to buy oil at the market?" Makir asked. He was surprised his mother would spend so much time making her own oil when she had so many other things to do.

"What oil? Tanak is not there today. They say he is working in his fields and plans to work straight through the night," she said. "He has no sons to serve in his place, you know. And they have no family goat or calves. I do not know how they are to survive such a burden as this. My only hope is that the gods will recognize Tanak's service and bring great blessings to his crops."

Sharai scraped the olives onto mats formed of tightly woven reeds and drained the oil from the slab into a small bowl. She placed the mats on top of the slab and began to roll a cylinder stone over them, extracting even more oil from the pulp.

"What would you like me to do, mother? My chores are through, and Filo has been grazed," Makir said.

"Where did you tie him? You know if harm were to befall him, we would have no cheese for our meals."

"He is in the shade at the corner of the market with the other goats," Makir replied. "Laotha is in charge of them. We will work in shifts, taking turns minding our animals, so that we have more time to help our families."

Makir felt sure this would make his mother proud and would definitely help his case with his father. Working in shifts had not been his idea, but still it could benefit him greatly. His mother always said, "The sign of a great man is in his ability to work well with others."

"I will need more olives," she said. "I am sure the community trees are picked dry by now, but perhaps you can find some that have fallen on the ground."

Makir nodded and grabbed a reed basket. Individual farmers owned much of Babylon, but there were still many fig and olive trees growing wild in the green valley. These could be harvested by anyone, but were most often used only by the poorest families of Babylon. Makir was a little embarrassed to be going to these fields, but his desire to please his mother was greater than his pride. He knew this embarrassment would quickly be forgotten once he held the honor of a craftsman.

When Makir got to the small cluster of trees in the middle of the great valley, he was surprised to see it crowded with other village children. Even Lystra was there! Maybe he could gain some favor with his friend after all. Perhaps this day wouldn't turn out quite so terrible.

Chapter 3

Jeremiah 29:12-13 "Then shall ye call upon Me, and ye shall go and pray unto Me, and I will hearken unto you. And ye shall seek Me, and find Me, when ye shall search for Me with all your heart."

It had been four days since the construction of the temple had begun and things in Makir's household were just beginning to settle down. There was much more work to be done for everyone, but they all seemed to settle into a routine. This morning, Makir stopped at the building site to watch the men work. He watched as they packed mud into rectangular molds. Other men stood at the furnace ready to bake the mud into stone.

Thousands of men worked fervently on the construction of the new temple. Makir could only see one of his brothers working, but all of the men in his family, besides himself and his father, had a job in the temple construction. Three of his older brothers were carriers. They were to bring the baked and cooled bricks to the building site where other men stacked the bricks in neatly slanted rows. Others smoothed and polished each brick until they glimmered in the sun. His oldest brother Esthu, now married and living with his own family, was a crew-boss. This was considered a position of great honor, though not as honorable as the men with the mathematical measurements. Still, it did hold great responsibility, and influence. He was to make sure everyone had the materials they needed and were all doing their jobs correctly.

Since Makir was considered too young to help with the actual construction of the temple, and the gods had not selected him to be a scribe, his days were spent doing tedious errands. If only he could help his father in his shop—his father still had not answered his request to do so, or go to the school for young scribes! Then everyone would look at him with the respect a young man deserved. As it was, everyone saw him as a child who only got in their way.

For this reason, Makir almost wished he could help with the construction. Only then would the men of the town see that he was capable of doing tasks that didn't involve mindless animals! Yet despite his desire for respect and his need to belong, he was actually relieved that he wasn't old enough to help. Something about this temple made him feel very nervous, as if it were terribly wrong.

"Hey, Makir! Catch!" Lystra ran up to him. He tossed a wad of cloth at him. Makir caught it with one hand.

"Think you can catch me?" Lystra yelled over his shoulder. He took off running. Makir chased after him, pumping his legs as fast as he could. They played this game often, and Lystra always won. Because he had the cloth, Makir was it. He aimed the wad at Lystra and threw it with as much force as he had. Lystra darted out of the way just in time. Lystra had the reflexes of a panther! Compared to him, Makir was like a sloth dangling from a limp branch. That was why Lystra liked to play this game. He loved the opportunity to show Makir just how superior he was. And inevitably, Makir was always it, and stayed it.

Desperately wanting this time to be different, Makir lunged for the cloth and scooped it off the ground. Gritting his teeth, he hurled the wad at Lystra a second time. It missed by at least four cubits! A group of girls nearby began to giggle and Makir could feel his face heat up.

"Come on," Makir said. "Let's go down to the river. My blood is about to burst through my skin!" He wiped the sweat from his face with his dusty hands. This was an excuse to stop the game and hopefully save some of his pride. Luckily, Lystra agreed and took off running towards the riverbank.

"Race you!" Lystra yelled as he sped off.

There was no way Makir could catch him, not only because Lystra had a head start, but also because he was the fastest kid in the city. Even so, Makir gave it his all. By the time they reached the edge of the west river, they were both gasping for air. Makir thought for sure he would puke he had run so hard. Besides being winded, Lystra seemed unaffected by the run. He wasted no time jumping in. Even though his lungs ached, Makir jumped in after him. The icy water soothed his tight, sun-baked skin. He plunged to the bottom and pressed his hands into the thick, smooth mud at the river floor.

"Lystra may be a better runner," Makir thought. "But I am like the great Leviathan in the deep water!"

To restore some of the pride he had lost in the race, Makir stayed under water until his lungs were ready to burst, just to prove he could. By the time he came up for air, Lystra was already getting out.

"I don't see why they don't let us help on the temple," Lystra said, pulling his body onto the riverbank.

"Surely we could do much better than old man Esteav!"

21

Lystra's voice cracked in mock imitation.

Makir forced an uneasy laugh. The gods would not be so pleased to hear such disrespect of a community elder. "Do you think this is such a good idea? This building?" Makir asked. He tried to sound casual, but his voice had a slight squeak to it.

"What do you mean?" Lystra snapped.

"I don't know. It just feels weird. Like they're doing something they're not supposed to, something scary."

Lystra burst out laughing and hurled a blob of mud at Makir. It splattered against Makir's shin like a giant, slimy slug. "Don't be such a tadpole!" he said. "You think you're smarter than the mighty Nimrod? You, a little reed of a boy, know better than the hunter of the great Behemoth? Nimrod is soon to become one of the great immortals, and he alone knows how to please the gods. When was the last time the gods spoke to you?"

"I was just--" Makir started to speak but Lystra cut him off.

"This temple will bring great honor to our city! We will become men of great renown, men who meet with the gods themselves. What could be scary about that?"

Makir shrugged. He stared at his feet and made small circles in the ground with his big toe. Now Lystra thought he was a fool. And maybe he was being foolish, letting his fearful nature control him. His father always said he thought too hard about things that should not be thought about. Tolah said some things were not to be understood, merely accepted. He said they were not to question their divine teachers, but were to merely honor and obey. The mysteries of the gods were for the priests to understand, not the common man. Yet Makir had a desire to know. He couldn't blindly believe in something he didn't understand.

Still, he knew he had a tendency to be fearful of new things.

22

Perhaps once the temple was built and life returned to normal, perhaps then he would feel more at ease. Everyone in Babylon believed in this temple. Surely they could not all be wrong!

"If you are to fear anything, you should fear the wrath of the gods should we cease building the temple," Lystra continued. "You heard what Nimrod said. If we don't build the temple, the gods will flood our land again. Then see who is afraid!"

"And what if he's wrong?" a voice behind them questioned.

Both boys jumped. Makir turned to see an old man standing propped against a gnarled old tree. He couldn't tell which was older, the tree or the man.

Both boys stared at him.

"What if Nimrod is wrong?" he asked again. "What if the sun and the moon really aren't gods at all? What if there is but one God, the Great Yahweh, what then?"

Makir laughed weakly, but his gut cramped. Lystra only sneered.

"Who are you?" Lystra snapped.

"Shem, son of Noah," the man replied.

Lystra made a snorting sound. His eyes contracted tightly.

"Yeah right! The man from the boat? The only boat in the world to survive the flood? That'd make you older than Babylon itself! Surely a man that old is losing his mind!" He turned to Makir. "Come on, Makir, this man's funny in the head."

Makir felt a deep urge to stay. He wanted to hear more, to learn who this man was and where he came from. He wanted to hear more about this Yahweh, but he knew that would be the end of his friendship with Lystra. And Lystra was his only friend. Sure, he was rude, and often got Makir into trouble, but what could Makir do about it? What was he supposed to do, hang out with the girls in the weaver's den? Or even worse, spend all his time alone? Feeling as if he had no choice but to follow Lystra, he gave the old man one last look and followed his friend back to the village.

Lystra talked the entire way, but Makir didn't hear much of what he said. He kept thinking about the man at the river. Could it really be the son of the legendary Noah? Supposedly, eight people had survived the flood, four men and their wives. According to legend, one man had headed north, and another had headed in the direction of the rising sun. Could some of them still be alive, and even more, living in Babylon? And if so, what had really caused the great flood that had washed all life from the land?

What was true? Was the flood the result of many angry jealous gods, or one great God called Yahweh? Did it even matter? Yes, yes it did matter. Something deep inside told him that the answer to that question would be the most important answer he would ever reach. But where could he get such answers?

"If you seek Me, you will find Me, if you seek Me with all your heart," a gentle voice whispered. It spoke directly to his heart, drawing him towards something, although he had no idea to what.

Chapter 4

Exodus 20:3-5 "Thou shalt have no other gods before Me. Thou shalt not make unto thee any graven image, or any likeness of any thing that is in heaven above, or that is in the earth beneath, or that is in the water under the earth: Thou shalt not bow down thyself to them, nor serve them: for I the Lord thy God am a jealous God, visiting the iniquity of the fathers upon the children unto the third and fourth generation of them that hate Me; and showing mercy unto thousands of them that love Me and keep My commandments."

"Makir, make yourself useful…if you wish to be a man. Ah, but you're still in the cloak of a child." Makir's brother Haron yanked at the young boy's tunic.

Makir's fists clenched. His ears and cheeks burned. His brother smirked, pleased at the reaction.

"Don't worry, my little flounder, there is work even for a fledgling like you." Haron shoved a large, smooth vessel into Makir's chest, nearly knocking him over. "Get us more clay. Quickly. If you can handle it."

Haron spun around, leaving Makir to stare angrily at the back of his head. Tears stung Makir's eyes and he could feel his hand tighten into small, tight fists. Why did his brother always mock him so? With a long breath, he wrapped his arms around the vessel and headed towards the edge of town.

"The air is a little thick today, wouldn't you say? Hear it's much worse up north. Sky's so grey can't remember the blue it used to be," a voice said.

Makir jumped. It was the man from the river. Even though he knew he needed to hurry, he had to stop. He needed to know more about this man and the strange things he talked of. He needed to know the truth!

"Wasn't always like this, you know. This dingy sky, scent of smoke in the air. Volcanoes erupting all the time."

The man sat cross-legged on the dry, dirt ground. A long brown beard, streaked with gray, reached from his chin to his lap. Thick eyebrows shielded his eyes from the intense afternoon sun. Makir stared at him for a minute, his mind racing so fast he couldn't keep up with his own thoughts. The longer he looked at this wrinkled old man, the more his heart burned within him. It was as if he held some treasure, some deep hidden treasure that Makir desperately needed. Makir needed to hear him speak, but what if someone saw him? What of Lystra? Makir inhaled sharply, looked around to make sure Lystra wasn't anywhere in sight, and then sat beside him.

"At one time, this world was a paradise, lush and green. The air was so pure and sweet it made a man feel strong as an ox. Just right for an old man's bones." He paused and rubbed his forehead in his hand. His eyes had a far-off, mournful look. After an uncomfortable silence, Shem continued. "Men didn't get so old back then. I don't quite understand it, but it's as if there's something causing us to age. It's almost as if the sun is stronger."

Makir stretched his arm out in front of him, staring at the tanned flesh. He looked up at Shem's creased face. He had heard talk of a world of no death, a land of paradise. But surely those were only fables told by old men and mothers.

The old man watched Makir intensely, his eyes piercing his heart. "Look around you. The world is dying. Everything is wearing down, failing."

The man looked out over the dry and cracking landscape. He watched the men at the building site for a while, a look of despair on his face. Then he turned to Makir with an intensity that sent chills along the boy's skin.

"This flood they talk about wasn't a pleasant filling of water, as a stream trickling into the pools. It was violent and destructive. Not only did it rain for forty days and nights, powerful waves roared across the earth, tearing it apart. Red-hot melted rock burst forth from open fissures in the earth, sending fire into the sky. When the blazing rocks touched the waters, powerful gusts of steam filled the air with dark ash and smoke. Our boat rocked violently. I thought for sure it would burst, that we'd all be torn to shreds!"

A picture of raging water and dark black skies filled Makir's mind. It would have been terrible! That is, if it was true.

"Hey, Makir!"

It was Lystra. Makir felt the blood drain from his face. He turned to see Lystra running towards him.

"Looks like you found yourself a friend, huh?" Lystra said with a laugh. He stood directly in front of Makir, his arms crossed tightly over his chest, a look of smug satisfaction on his face.

Makir's mouth went dry. If only he could crawl into the dirt and hide! What could he say to stop Lystra's mocking? Knowing there was no way to excuse himself, he stood up slowly and brushed the dirt from his tunic with precise, deliberate motions. He hoped he was portraying more confidence than he felt. If Lystra knew how foolish he felt, Makir would never hear the end of it. He looked Lystra dead in the eye when he spoke.

"I was just resting," he said.

This wasn't entirely false. Before Lystra could ask him anything else, Makir grabbed the clay vase and headed towards the river. He hoped Lystra would leave him alone, but Lystra was having too much fun to be diverted. He followed at Makir's heels, taunting.

"Makir's got a friend! Makir's got a friend, a crazy old, lazy old, grumpy old friend!"

Makir gritted his teeth. His cheeks burned. He spun around and glared at Lystra. "Knock it off!" he spat. "What will the gods think of your disrespect for a city elder?"

"Who him?" Lystra asked. "You call him an elder? After what he said about the gods, they will be greatly honored by my actions! Besides, that man's as crazy as a jackal, and I bet his madness has gotten into you!" Lystra burst out laughing. "The demons got a hold of your head! Next thing you know, you'll be drooling out of the side of your face, just like the old man back there." Lystra sagged his face to one side and hunched his body forward in mockery. As he walked, he dragged one foot behind, his knees turning in.

Makir looked back at the old man in shame. The man caught his eye and held his gaze with a look that sent a stab to Makir's heart. It was a sad, almost knowing look, as if this was what he had expected.

28

Lystra's voice continued, endlessly drilling at Makir's nerves. It took all Makir's determination to tune him out. He forced his thoughts in a new direction; deliberately focusing on the conversation he had had with the old man. He had heard of this Yahweh before, when he was a young boy and spent most of his time with his mother. The old women had told him stories of the first God of the world, a God of a power and might that none has surpassed. But then, according to the stories, something happened. Somehow, this God, the one they called the Great I Am, quit being told of. He had been replaced in their hearts and minds by other gods, the gods of the city and land. What had happened to this Yahweh?

"I, even I, am the LORD; and beside me there is no Savior. Before the day was I am He. Before Me there was no god formed, neither shall there be after Me." These words flooded his mind and seemed to surround him on every side. He felt a gentle breeze pass over him.

Makir and Lystra walked up the side of the valley to the west river, the hot sun burning into their back like a flame. Makir stared absently at the land ahead, his mind going in so many directions; his thoughts soon became one big jumble.

"What is wrong with you?" Lystra asked sharply. He was staring at Makir with a look of intrigued amusement.

Makir's cheeks burned. "I was just thinking," he said.

He was in no mood to go another round with Lystra. Hoping he would leave him alone, Makir walked with his gaze locked on the ground in front of him. The path to the river was rocky and bare, worn down by years of passage. The red dirt was cracked from lack of water and the heat of the sun. They were due for another flooding soon. The skies were often dry in Babylon, and the whole land would have perished long ago if it hadn't been for the regular flooding of the rivers. This flooding brought life to the valley, creating a small strip of green in the middle of an immense desert.

Fiery mountains erupted in the distance, filling the sky with a brownish-gray haze. The top of the horizon was dotted with small specks of red and orange as melted rock exploded from the ground. When old men shared their stories of the land with the red river, a river so hot and fierce it turned layers of stone into liquid smooth as honey and sent the strongest trees crashing to the ground, Makir's imagination would take over. He liked to pretend that he alone had traveled to the land of the belching earth and had climbed the steep mountain slopes to peer inside their fiery bellies. In his mind, he scaled the mounds upon mounds of black rock and leapt across the freshly cut canyons. He was a mighty hunter in search of the great lizards, and he alone had found their hiding place.

"So, you gonna' fill that thing or what?" Lystra asked. His voice had a mocking tone to it.

Makir was embarrassed to realize how distracted he had gotten. How long had he been standing there? In Babylon, by the age of eight you were supposed to be through with childish dreams and games, but Makir wasn't ready to leave his dream world behind. If only his distractions didn't get him into so much trouble. Like now. He had gotten so distracted by his thoughts he couldn't even remember why he had come here in the first place.

"Your brother's not going to be too happy at how long it's been taking you to get clay. What if they have all run out? The gods themselves will burn with fury at your lack of respect." He raised his arms to the sky. "The one job they give you, and you fail! It's like you don't even care! Did you forget what this temple is for? Who it is for?"

Makir could have told Lystra to jump into the river! He knew the builders would have plenty of clay. They had people who spent their entire day running to and from the river to get more supplies. That was all they did. The only reason Haron had asked Makir to do it was so that he could tell Makir what to do. Not because he really needed it! Makir wanted to tell Lystra to mind his own business, but he bit his lip to keep from saying something he would regret.

Makir bent down and began to scoop the soft, wet clay into the vessel. He traced his fingers along the smooth, even layers of pink and tan, bringing the colors together into delicate swirls and curves. Each layer sat perfectly on top of the other, as if they had all been poured from a great pot just like the ones in his father's shop. Ten feet ahead, the fast moving current broke and slowed against round, shiny rocks, leaving foaming bubbles in its wake. He watched the steadily moving stream tug urgently at the river's bank, creating smooth twists and turns in the sand. A large chunk of rock tore off its base and rolled downstream until it rested in a gentle pool at Makir's feet.

Makir reached out and touched it, rubbing the gritty grains between his thumb and index finger. It turned to powder in his hands. This was the same clay they used to make the bricks for the temple; only they made theirs stronger by laying the clay in the red flame.

Makir loved to create things from the smooth soil and often came to the river's edge when his daily chores were done. He could create wonderful, multilayer dens with many rooms. He even made streets and spiral staircases using small sticks and flat river stones. Once he had even made a great Behemoth, round scales and all. If only he could stay at the river all day, but he knew he couldn't. Today he had a job to do. For once. He couldn't risk messing it up. Word could get back to his father: then he'd never be able to help in the metal shop!

Makir knew he had taken way too much time at the river. He would have to hurry if he hoped to avoid his brother's anger. He grabbed the clay vessel and ran as fast as he could back to the city, leaving Lystra, and his mocking voice, far behind. By the time he got to the center of Babylon, he felt as if his lungs were going to burst. To catch his breath, he stopped and leaned against some cooled brick. As he watched the men work on the tower Nimrod had ordered to be built, he thought of all the things the old man at the river had told him. He wondered what went through their minds. Why were they building this temple? Did they believe in it as strongly as Makir's father, or were they only doing what they thought was expected of them? Did any of them think about it at all?

The builders sang and chanted as they worked. It was a song to the gods, one that was sung often during feasts and new moon festivals. They were pledging their allegiance and asking the gods to bless their work. Everyone worked with great enthusiasm, even the old men. Their jobs were less intense, and perhaps, more honorable. They were given leadership roles that required little if any heavy lifting. The more strenuous jobs, such as bringing the large stones from the furnace to the building site, were left to the younger men.

As the stones were piled higher and higher, a crew of men brought in great quantities of sand to fill the temple floor. They would pile the sand until it reached the top of the uppermost layer. That way the builders would have something to stand on when they added more levels. Eventually the sandy floor would reach all the way to the last level only to be emptied out again, layer by layer, once the temple was completed. Then, all that would remain would be the smooth dirt floor.

Makir watched as young women ran from man to man, water-filled vessels on their heads and in their hands. One by one, empty water skins were filled. Some men lifted the vases above their mouths and let the water drip onto their tongues and down their throats. A man could dehydrate quickly in the open sun and needed to drink often. Makir was glad his sisters were back at the ovens, close to his mother. They weren't allowed to help her until after their six dashes were up, but they would be close enough to come if an emergency were to arise with baby Mila.

A group of young children ran carelessly down the street, giggling as they went. They were engaged in some game, although Makir couldn't quite tell what it was. He looked at them longingly. How he wanted to join them, to let all his thoughts of the temple and Babylon drift away into a world of make-believe.

"Makir! Where have you been?" Haron's voice snapped.

Makir jumped. His brother was coming toward him, his eyes fierce. They held a spark of pleasure, of cruel satisfaction, as if he felt great joy in seeing Makir fail.

Makir turned his face toward the ground and waited for his brother's angry words. Haron grabbed the vessel from him and spun around, his lips turning up at the corners.

"I knew you couldn't do it," he said.

Chapter 5

John 10:27-28 "My sheep hear My voice, and I know them, and they follow Me: and I give them eternal life; and they shall never perish, neither shall any man pluck them out of My hand."

Heat radiated from Makir's sweaty skin. He slumped against the rock behind him and watched Haron walk back to the building site. Everyone seemed to have a job of great importance. Everyone had a purpose. Everyone but him. His only purpose was to care for a mindless goat!

"Your purpose is in Me," whispered a voice.

Makir looked around to see who was speaking, even though he knew this voice spoke not to his ears, but to his heart.

"Who are you?" his mind replied.

"I made you, and you are Mine. If you seek Me, you will find Me, if you seek me with all your heart."

Those words surrounded him, pulled him and filled him with a longing he had never felt before. It was as if there was an emptiness inside him, a deep hole, calling to be filled.

A raspy voice caught his attention. "Man is just as evil now as he was before the flood," the voice said.

Makir spun around to see who was speaking to him. It was the man from the river, the man named Shem. He stood beside him, as if he had suddenly appeared. It was almost as if this man had been following him, or perhaps had been sent to him. The thought of this brought chills to Makir's spine.

"Seems we always want to reject our Creator and worship His creation instead. We want to make our own rules, our own gods, gods that fit our own desires so that we can do whatever we want. No one wants a God who has rules and penalties."

Makir thought about this. He thought about the tower Nimrod was having the town build. Was that what he was doing? Making his own gods so that he could live however he wanted? And what of his claims? Claims that he could transform into a god himself?

He looked back at the men building the temple. The men worked in rhythm to their chanting. Bakal stood on top of the tiered steps, his face taking on the look of a crazed panther. As the chants grew louder, the men's motions seemed to grow more and more intense and forceful.

Makir turned back to Shem, but the old man was gone. Angry and confused, he turned his face to the sky. "If You're there, show me!" his heart cried out.

He held his breath and waited. The sky was motionless, just an endless blue as far as the eye could see. Did he really believe some supernatural Being would be able to read his thoughts? And even more, would actually respond? If this Yahweh really did exist, and if He really was the Supreme and Only God, surely He had better things to do than waste his time on some worthless boy from the land between the two rivers! Yet even as these thoughts filled his mind, deep in his heart he had a sense that this God had heard him. Somehow, some deep, almost subconscious part of him knew there was a God somewhere who did hear him, who knew him, and perhaps wanted to be known in return.

Overwhelmed by the thought, Makir decided to go home and see if his mother needed any help. What he needed was something to keep him busy. Perhaps if he didn't have so much time on his hands perhaps then he wouldn't spend so much time worrying about things that didn't make any sense to him.

As he began walking back to his small, mud-packed den, his feet began to lag. He felt as if a thick fog had crept into his ears and filled his head. Suddenly his house seemed terribly far away. And he was exhausted, not only physically, but mentally as well.

As he neared his house, he took a deep breath and forced his back to straighten. He paused just outside the doorway, took another deep breath, and put on a big, although tight, smile. He waited for his heart to slow and then entered the house with as much enthusiasm and cheerfulness as he could manage.

His baby sister Mila sat in the center of the room playing with some dolls his mother had made from old ragged cloth. The minute she saw him, she threw the dolls aside and hurried over to Makir. Her small thick body rocked back and forth on her round, flat feet as she toddled across the room.

"Mokka! Mokka! Mokka home!" she cried out. Her tiny hands pulled onto his legs as if she were trying to climb up into his arms. "Mokka play! Mokka play!"

He tussled her hair and tickled her sides, but his thoughts bounced through his head like caged locusts. That voice, that deep, yet silent voice, replayed again and again until he thought his head would burst.

"I made you. You are mine. I made you. I made you."

His mother sat hunched over a stone mortar and pestle, grinding grain into flour. She looked up when Makir walked into the room. "We are out of figs," she said.

This meant that Makir needed to go and get more. The fig tree bore its fruit twice a year and now was the best time for picking. These trees grew in a small cluster just a few feet from the east river. Makir would have preferred a job that would have allowed him to stay in the cool mud house, but he knew better than to complain. At least it would give him something to do. Anyway, if he was lucky, he would find some fresh berries to eat along the way.

Not wanting to be given any more tasks, but still wanting to please his parents, Makir took as much time as possible making his way to the fig trees. Once there, he lay on the warm ground and stared up at the sky above him. The sound of the softly running river and the warmth of the sun soothed his frazzled mind. He closed his eyes and breathed in the sweet scent of sun-ripened figs. Birds twittered around him, pecking at the rotting fruit scattered along the ground. A gentle breeze rustled his hair against his face.

He must have fallen asleep, for he was jolted awake by a falling fig. He immediately sprang to a sitting position. How long had he slept? Worried that perhaps he had slept quite awhile, he quickly gathered the figs he had been sent for and ran back towards home.

By the time Makir entered the city, the sun was low in the sky. It burned reddish brown behind thick layers of black and grey smoke-filled clouds. Occasionally, you could see sparks fly in the distance as volcanoes continued to erupt. Tired from the heavy load he carried, and the thick, smothering air, he leaned against the wall of the nearest shelter. It belonged to Nimrod. Makir could hear voices coming from the window above.

"You are brilliant, my fine man. I never thought it would work," a deep voice said.

"I knew it would work," came the reply. "The people don' want to believe in Yahweh anymore. He's too demanding. Rigid All they needed was an excuse to go their own way. That's why they love me so much. I gave them the excuse they needed."

Makir recognized Nimrod's voice but couldn't identify the voice of the other man. Surely it was one of Nimrod's many loyal priests. There were at least twenty holy men serving directly under him and nearly ten priestesses who attended to the priests' needs.

"That you did, Nimrod. That you did. And setting yoursel up as a world leader in the process. Do you really think it wil work?" the man asked.

"It is working. They already believe in my 'gods,'" Nimrod said. "They've already rejected their faith. They are like smooth silt in my hands. As soon as the temple is complete, and they are confident of my deity, nothing will be impossible for me! I will rule the world!"

Makir couldn't believe what he was hearing. Was it really that easy to fool people? Could it be true that they allowed this deception, even welcomed it? And this Yahweh, could that be the same God that Shem talked about? If so, surely this Yahweh wouldn't let Nimrod's plans succeed. He wouldn't allow people to ignore Him and forget Him entirely, would He? The thought of what Yahweh might do scared him, yet the thought of Him doing nothing scared him even more. Forcing these thoughts out of his mind, Makir returned his attention to the men above him.

"And you think this too will work?"

"Open your eyes, man. I have them building the tower so high, they will believe it reaches all the way to heaven. Then I wil ell them that heaven itself comes down to meet with me, to become a part of me." Nimrod laughed and then continued. "After all the hours they have put into this project, they will have to believe me. Even if they don't, they will convince themselves it is true. They won't want to think that all their time, energy and gifts have been a waste. Don't you see, I get them involved bit by bit, turning their minds and hearts so gradually, they won't even realize it until it's too late. By the time I am done, the only thing they will be able to do is to worship me."

"As I said before, Nimrod, you are brilliant. I only hope you remember to cut me in on the riches. Setting me up with my own kingdom would be appreciated," the man said.

"Of course, of course. We will create so many gods for the people to worship, you can be any of your choosing, so long as you don't outshine me. We would hate to have the sun cease shining, wouldn't we?"

Both men laughed. Makir felt like he was going to throw up. He couldn't believe what he was hearing. That old man, Shem, had been right all along! These other gods Nimrod talked about were nothing more than the inventions of men!

"I better get back to the temple, see how the men are coming along. I will report back at sundown."

Makir heard footsteps above him. It would only be seconds before the man was down. He quickly grabbed his bulging sack and sprinted toward the building site before the men could see him.

Nimrod's evil voice filled his mind, his words repeating again and again. Makir pressed his palms against his ears and pinched his eyes shut. His world seemed to be spinning out of control. What was he going to do? What could he do?

"Whoa, boy! What's gotten into you? The sun got you sick

or something?"

Haron wiped the sweat from his brow. He stood staring at his younger brother, a look of genuine concern on his face. Makir could only stare at him in reply. He didn't know what to say. If he told Haron what he had heard, his brother would never believe him. And why should he? After all, he was only a kid. Besides, Haron looked up to Nimrod and obeyed his every word. He believed in him, and this temple. He was proud of it. They all were. And now they were almost done. They would never accept that it had all been a lie.

"I don't have time to wait for you to catch your tongue. Give me a fig and get out of here." Haron snatched a handful of figs and headed back to the molding and baking site.

Makir watched him leave for a few minutes, then turned and walked away. He felt as if he had to concentrate on every step. Everything was so confusing. He needed to talk to someone, but who would listen? Who would ever believe him?

"I will not turn you away. Whoever comes to Me, I will never turn away," a voice said. It spoke directly to his heart and touched his very soul.

"Where are you?" Makir yelled up at the sky.

As soon as the words exploded out of his mouth, he felt foolish. He held his breath and waited for some taunting remark but what he heard made his blood run cold.

Voices rose behind him. They were angry, panicked voices, yet for some reason, he couldn't understand what they were saying. It was as if they were all speaking a different tongue. He turned to see men yelling at one another, faces red, arms waving in the air. Had everyone gone mad? Did this have anything to do with that temple they were building? Could this be the hand of Yahweh?

He had to find the old man! He took off running back towards the city center. It didn't take long to find him. The old man was standing in the middle of the dirt packed road, staring up at the sky with his arms raised. He looked happy. Why would he look happy? Was the man out of his mind? Were they all losing their minds?

Makir ran up to the old man and stood directly in front of him, his eyes searching the old man's face.

"What's going on?" Makir meant to ask, but what came out instead shook him to the core. It was nothing more than a strange jumble of sounds. In his mind, his words were the same, but the sounds his mouth produced were foreign to him. And yet, they made sense despite their foreignness. Shem's eyes locked on his with an expression of such knowing, such certainty, Makir's mouth went dry. He backed away slowly, his eyes blurred with tears. Shem stared at him for a few more minutes then turned his attention back to the sky, his arms once again raised. Makir turned and ran.

He didn't stop running until he had reached his small den. It was empty. Dark. He stood in the center of the cold mud house and stared straight ahead, not seeing anything at all.

Chapter 6

Hosea 7:13-14 "Woe unto them! For they have fled from Me: destruction unto them; because they have transgressed against Me: though I have redeemed them, yet they have spoken lies against Me. And they have not cried unto Me with their heart, when they howled upon their beds: they assembled themselves for corn and wine, and they rebel against Me."

Makir's mother burst into the room. Mila toddled frantically behind her wailing, her tiny fingers grasping for her mother in fearful desperation. Sharai's eyes were wild. She looked at her son with a look of such pleading and terror; Makir felt the blood drain from his head.

"Crazy! It's all crazy! All of them," she shrieked. Her voice was shrill.

Makir was amazed he could understand her. She didn't speak the way she used to, but somehow her words made sense to him. It took a moment for this to register. Not knowing what to say, he nodded weakly. Her body slacked when she realized he understood

Tears ran down her cheeks. In one moment, she lunged at him and pressed him against herself. She shook with tears. Eventually, her loud sobbing settled into a quiet whimper and her grasp on Makir relaxed. She pushed him an arm's length away and scanned his face. Baby Mila clawed at Sharai's legs and skirt, her wailing growing louder and more desperate. Her cries fell on deaf ears.

"It's all craziness, I tell you. Everything. All of them. The gods have gone mad! They made us crazy!" Sharai cried. "It's a curse! A horrible, evil curse!"

Makir stared at her for a minute. The room seemed to close in around him. It was as if he were watching her from far away. She looked so frightened and helpless; so alone. Completely and utterly alone. Seeing her that way, desperate, frail…mortal, made everything else so clear. Suddenly, it all made sense.

"No, mom, not the gods, but God." Makir spoke with a courage and authority he didn't know he possessed. He couldn't explain it, he didn't even understand it, but he knew it was true. Deep inside, he knew this God.

"There's only one God," Makir said. "The Creator of the land, earth and sea. He made the sun, moon and stars. He did this because of our sin. We have forgotten Him and are worshipping His creation instead."

Sharai slapped him hard across the face, sending him sprawling backwards. He stared at her in shock. His little sister went silent. She stared at her mother with a blank face and then ran to Makir. She wrapped her arms around his leg and began to wail once again. Sharai stared at them both, her eyes burning with anger. She backed away slowly.

"How dare you, you evil child!" Sharai spat. "It's all your fault, you blasphemous boy! You made the gods angry, and it is because of you their fury burns against all of us!" Her eyes contracted sharply and her entire body tensed. Makir had never seen her so angry before. He cringed and inched backward towards the wall behind him. Suddenly the room felt very cold.

At that moment his father burst into the den. He looked from his wife, to his son, then back outside. Sharai ran into her husband's arms, her sobs returning. He placed his hand around the back of her head, his eyes wide and blank.

"Oh, Tolah, we are cursed! We are all cursed, and it's our fault! Because of this evil child of ours, our people will be utterly destroyed."

Tolah jerked away from her.

"Makir's fault? How could you ever say such a thing? He's our boy! How can one small boy cause such chaos to an entire land?"

"He--"

Tolah put up his hand. His gaze was as hard as stone. "I will not hear another word!" his voice boomed. "How can you curse the fruit of your womb?"

"He denied the gods, Tolah!" Sharai cried. "He said that they were not gods! He called them mere creations of some other God. The gods heard his blasphemies. Now we are all being punished!"

"Shhhh. Even the gods can see he is just a boy. A few chants and sacrifices, and all will be forgotten. There must be some other answer, you will see. This is the work of demons, I am sure. We must seek the favor of the gods, and have the demons purged from our land."

Sharai calmed down enough to listen, but her voice still trembled when she spoke. "Do you really think so?"

"Yes, my love. Everything will be fine. I promise. I will

ind Nimrod. He will know what to do. He will make everything right again."

Makir's stomach rolled. He had to stop him! Nimrod had done enough as it was! He had to tell his father the truth!

"Father, wait! Please!"

Tolah frowned and made a jerking motion with his hand, as if shoving Makir aside, then hurried out the door. Makir's mother crumpled to the floor, her face pressed in her hands. She wept quietly.

Seconds later, Haron ran into the room. He took one look at his mother's tear stained face, and then ran out again.

Makir didn't know what to do. He didn't want to stay and watch his mother cry, but he didn't have anywhere else to go. The air inside felt thick and heavy. The thought of going out in the open air, surrounded by all the yelling people with jumbled, chaotic sounds scared him, but he knew if he didn't get fresh air soon, he would pass out. Forcing his numb legs to move, he walked out.

Once outside, he took a deep breath. He let it out slowly, trying to calm the pounding in his chest. He felt lightheaded. The noise surrounded him on every side, ringing in his ears like cymbals. Men ran in every direction. Women followed behind them, wailing.

"Now what? Now what? Yahweh, where are you? What am I to do?" his heart pleaded. "What am I to do now?"

"If you seek Me, you will find Me. I am right here," came the reply.

It was the same voice he had heard before. What did that mean? How could he seek someone he couldn't see? And how could this Yahweh be right here, yet not be visible?

"But where?" he yelled at the sky. "How? I don't know where you are!"

"Neb Te-ner humet! Neb Te-ner humet," a man yelled as he ran past. He grasped at the air in front of him, as if he was trying to grab on to something. He kept repeating the words again and again and although Makir didn't understand them, it was as if the man was asking for help.

Makir couldn't take it anymore. Surely his head would explode if he heard one more muddled cry. He squeezed his hands against his ears and raced to the river. He didn't stop running until he felt the cool water touch the tips of his feet. Hot tears streamed down his cheeks. Nothing made sense anymore. There was nowhere to go. There was no one to help, no one he could trust.

"I will never leave you nor forsake you," the voice repeated. By now he had learned to recognize this as Yahweh's voice. It wasn't a voice he heard with his ears, but instead, with his heart. Knowing that this God was speaking to him should have brought him great fear, but for some reason he couldn't understand, it brought him comfort.

"What do you want me to do?" Makir responded.

"Trust me. Blessed are they that wait on the Lord. Be still and know that I am God," came the reply.

"But how can I be still when everything around me is falling apart?" Makir cried out.

There was no response. What did that mean, wait on the Lord? Wait for what? More confusion? More destruction?

Makir grabbed a handful of stones and hurled them at the river in front of him. The water splashed against his legs, but he barely felt it. He stared at the circular patterns made by the plunging rocks and sank down to sit against the muddied bank. Countless thoughts spun around and around in his head. His mind was going in so many directions. He hardly knew what to believe. What was once truth, was now a complete lie, and what he had never heard of before was now the only thing he knew to be true. Exhausted, he let his mind go with the gently tugging current, focusing all his thoughts on the steady flow of water in front of him.

By the time Makir headed back to his shelter, the moon was beginning to rise. The shouts that had filled the city earlier had been replaced by weak whimpers. Men talked in hushed, soothing voices, probably trying to bring comfort to their families. Their words were meaningless to him.

His own house was no different, except that for some odd reason, he could understand what they were saying. His mother still sat crouched in the corner, just as she had been when he had left hours before. Her eyes were red and swollen, but the tears had stopped. His father's voice echoed in the small mud home.

"Nimrod is nothing more than a coward and a fraud! If he were truly a god, he would help his people!" Tolah said. "He would make his words known to us, but I couldn't understand a thing he said. The demons have gotten him, as well! It's as if we've all gone dumb and mute."

Tolah's eyes had a wild, frantic look to them. "The words I once spoke with great ease now refuse to come," he said. "Instead, strange sounds I've never heard before come out in their place. Everyone speaks their own tongue. A tongue for every household, but only that household can understand the words."

"I don't understand it, my husband," Sharai replied. "How can we understand one another, but not understand those outside our home? This seems like some terrible, weird dream."

"If it is a dream," said Tolah, "then it is a nightmare we share. The whole city is in chaos."

Makir had a difficult time falling asleep that night. Angry voices echoed throughout the town as families fought with one another. Yet his home was painfully silent. They were all afraid to speak, terrified at the sound of their own words. Makir longed for his mother to hold him, to gently run her fingers through his hair and tell him everything would be okay. He needed her to tell him she still loved him, but she hadn't spoken to him all evening, and whenever she looked at him, the anger in her eyes cut Makir's heart so deeply he thought it would break. Even Tolah was cold and distant. Normally his father was his strong tower, a man who could bring peace to every situation, but tonight he was so upset, he hardly realized Makir was in the room. Makir stared at the roof above him, his heart pleading for comfort.

"Where are you now, Yahweh?" his heart cried. "I need you. I need you now."

If there was a response, Makir couldn't hear it over his own despair. Eventually, he fell into a restless sleep.

The next morning, Makir awoke to silence. The crying had stopped. There were no more yells, no more wailing women. He was amazed to see his father already up and getting ready for work as if it were any other day.

Sharai pulled herself up on her mat and watched her husband in silence. She wrapped a thickly woven cloth around her shoulders. She shivered against the dense fabric despite the stale warmth of the room. As Makir watched her, he was suddenly aware of just how old she was. In fact, she seemed to have aged greatly since the night before, and once again, Makir was reminded of her frailty. Slowly, the others in the room began to stir awake.

"You go to work?" Sharai asked. Her voice was flat, lifeless.

"I must," was all Tolah said.

48

Bakal started to get up, gave his father a puzzled look and then lay back down. Tolah didn't respond. He looked at his wife one last time, grabbed a handful of fig cakes left over from the day before and left. Makir watched him go with a renewed sense of hope. Could the nightmare be over? Had Yahweh drawn back his hand?

Sharai walked slowly to the coals that lay smoldering in the hearth and stirred them to rekindle their flame. As the flame grew, she grabbed a handful of crushed grain, a lump of white fat and a few plump figs from the vessel Makir had gathered the day before. Kneeling over a smooth, flat stone, she began to knead them into thin cakes. She placed another flat stone on top of the burning coals and went back to her kneading. Once the stone was hot, she poured a few drops of olive oil onto the center of the heated stone. It began to sizzle and hiss, filling the room with the sweet smell of roasting olives. Next, she placed the flattened cakes in the hot oil and let them cook to a golden brown.

As the aroma of wheat and figs filled the room, Makir realized how incredibly hungry he was. He hadn't eaten much the night before. No one had. As his brothers began to rise and make their way to the center of the room, Makir realized they were just as hungry as he was. They sat cross-legged on the floor, their knees only a hand's width apart. His mother handed the plate of steaming bread to his oldest sister who in turn handed this to Bakal. Makir's stomach rolled and cramped as he waited for the plate to be passed to him.

Siseral, the most dutiful of all his sisters, filled a jug with warm, fermented barley. She also handed this to Bakal. With Tolah gone, Bakal stood as head of house and was honored as such by having first pick of the meal. Next, a large chunk of goat cheese was passed. Each family member tore off a piece then passed the rest along.

Normally, meals were a time of great cheer and festivities, and each family member shared stories from the previous day with one another, but today they all ate in silence. After the plate had been passed around more times than was needed, it was finally placed in the center of the circle.

No one moved. They all lingered around the dirtied dishes not quite knowing what to do. So much of their day had been centered around the temple, around serving Nimrod. Without this they were lost. And Tolah had left no instructions.

Chapter 7

Romans 1:19-20 "Because that which may be known of God is manifest in them; for God hath shown it unto them. For the invisible things of Him from the creation of the world are clearly seen, being understood by the things that are made, even His eternal power and Godhead, so that they are without excuse."

Bakal stood up. "We will go to the temple," he said. "A sacrifice must be made."

Makir felt the blood drain from his face. Hadn't they learned anything the night before? He watched with growing fear as his other brothers rose to their feet. They nodded their heads in agreement, a look of determination and resolve on their faces, as if this were the only logical thing for them to do. The women rose as well and began to clean up the discarded food. Makir watched them all in shocked disbelief. Everyone moved around him in a blur, their voices rising and falling like dripping water.

"Makir!" Sharai snapped. "Follow your brothers!" Her words were filled with venom. It was the first time she had spoken his name since the angry words of the previous day.

Makir jumped to his feet and raced after his brothers. His eyes narrowed in on the jumble of dirtied feet in front of him, as if this would keep his own feet steady.

"Yahweh, if you are really there, please help me," he silently pleaded.

A cool breeze blew over him, bringing with it a feeling of strength and peace. Makir could almost feel his fears begin to lift, as if a dark cloud had been removed. He could almost feel someone walking beside him, holding him, guiding him. And suddenly, it was as if a large veil covering his eyes had been removed, and he was able to see the world clearly for the first time. He looked out at the sun just beginning to peer over the horizon and felt as if he too were just beginning to dawn.

The smell of animal fat drifted from earthen windows as they passed the other dwellings. The men of the city were filing out of their homes, their eyes set on the path ahead of them. A few of them had birds of varying sizes flung over their shoulders. The birds had their beaks and feet bound and their wings were tied tightly to their plump bellies. It was obvious they were heading to the temple as well.

"Now what, Yahweh? I don't want to dishonor You in this way." Makir said.

What would he do if his brothers asked him to share in the sacrifice? Would he be strong enough to stand up for Yahweh? And if he did, would their anger towards him be as strong as his mother's had been? Would it be worse? Would they want to kill him?

"I will never leave you nor forsake you," Yahweh answered.

Makir repeated those words to himself again and again as he followed his brothers. "He will never leave me nor forsake me. He will never leave me nor forsake me." This was a promise he would hold on to with every part of his being.

Every time he repeated those words, his fears would lessen. His fears didn't leave entirely. He knew he could very likely face death, but at least he knew he did not have to go through this alone.

When they got to the city center, men were already crowded around the temple building site. All building efforts had been abandoned. Large square stones lay scattered along the ground where they had been hastily dropped and left. Globs of clay hardened along the outside of half-filled molds. Tools littered the ground, causing the men to trip as they angrily swarmed the cluttered site, shoving one another, fists pounding in the air.

Makir scanned the area. Nimrod was nowhere to be seen. Half the priests were gone and none of the priestesses were in sight. The few priests who did remain had barricaded themselves behind the larger stones. They stood on top of one of the highest steps and stared at the angry mob in front of them. Fear filled their eyes. The men pressed in around them, pushing and shoving, pressing one another against the pale white rocks that separated the men from the priests.

Makir and his brothers stood on the outer edges of the crowd and stared at the mob in front of them. Bakal started to lunge forward, his fists clenched at his sides, but Haron pulled him back. Another man, one of Tolah's friends, stepped up and held Bakal by the right shoulder. Haron maintained a firm grip on his left arm. Bakal fought to get loose for a while, but the hold on him only strengthened. Eventually, he gave up. For a moment, his eyes met Makir's and Makir was surprised to see it wasn't anger that burned in Bakal's eyes, but fear. Makir had never seen Bakal afraid of anything. He couldn't bear to hold his gaze and so he quickly turned away to watch the men in front of him.

One of the priests, a man with the face and build of a child stepped forward and spoke to the crowd. "Ayshe'a', menare-ona!" he said. His voice rang out loudly, but his confidence was betrayed by a quivering in his tone. His words were nothing more than a mix of meaningless sounds and phrases.

The minute the mob heard his unintelligible words, they picked up stones and began to hurl them at the priests. The priests crowded close together and crouched low to the ground as the stones flew all around them. They scurried backwards, their feet slipping in the sand, their hands clutching at the loose soil behind them as they tried to pull themselves away from the mob and hurling stones. The stones were flying with such fury it was as if a thunderstorm had erupted. Some of the younger men, three and four of them together, tried to pick up the heavy boulders that lay scattered across the ground.

The men were ruled by their anger and hatred. Makir couldn't bear to watch anymore. Wanting to get as far from all the anger and hatred as possible, he ran as fast as he could in the opposite direction.

"Oh, Yahweh, what now? Yahweh, what will we do now?" he cried.

The road ahead blurred with tears. The angry faces from the temple swirled around in his mind. He could still hear their enraged voices and the sound of the stones hitting the ground. Without thinking, he ran to the water's edge, flung himself upon the muddied bank and sobbed.

"In repentance and rest is your salvation. In quietness and trust is your strength," Yahweh whispered.

Even though Makir didn't fully understand what this meant,

he knew he needed this God. More than anything in the world, he needed Yahweh. He couldn't do this alone anymore. The emptiness in his heart consumed him and called to be filled, to be filled with this God. In that instant, he had a sudden realization of Yahweh's holiness, and in the light of such perfect glory, he realized just how unworthy he was. Seeing the holiness of God brought him to his knees. Unable to do anything else, he gave to Yahweh his very self, all his fears and sorrows, all his hopes and dreams. Kneeling in the dirt, his head bowed low in humility, he poured out a heartfelt response.

"My God and King, I don't know You very well, but I want to know You more," he cried. "I am so unworthy of You! I am just as evil and selfish as all these men around me. Please forgive me for my selfishness. Make me clean. Please help me to do better, to live for you and not for the opinions of man. I want to please You! Show me who You are! Help me to do what You want," he prayed.

A warm breeze blew over him and filled his very soul. In an instant, the emptiness was gone, and in its place there was a joy and peace he had never felt before. For the first time in his life, he felt complete, whole. He would never be alone again.

He stayed at the river for the rest of the day, and went back often in the following weeks. The time spent there became his source of strength. Things had gotten better in Babylon, but the city was still in turmoil. People were calmer, but the anger was still there. Only now it was hidden behind stoic faces and dull eyes.

It was becoming more and more difficult for the people to live amongst one another. Families were quickly running out of food. Because the shoppers and merchants were unable to communicate with one another at the market, all bargaining had stopped. And now, the market itself was bare. Men had gathered their goods and abandoned their booths. Craftsmen had closed their doors, realizing that without the words to bargain with, their goods were useless. Many had resorted to stealing.

Today he sat in the quiet of his darkened home, pondering all these things in his heart. What would Yahweh do next? What would Yahweh have him do? Before he could think much farther, his father's voice interrupted his thoughts.

"Makir, go with your brothers to the river. We need more fish," Tolah said.

"But father, the river is empty. Its banks are covered with men, and their rods only come up empty. Why should we have any more luck?" Makir asked.

"Go!" Tolah yelled.

Makir jumped to his feet reflexively. It was the first time he had ever heard his father yell. Silence fell over the entire house. All Makir heard was the pounding of his own heart, beating in his chest like a drum. Bakal grabbed Makir by the arm and pulled him out of the house.

Makir and his brothers walked single file down to the river's edge. It brought Makir great sadness to see his place of retreat so crowded with men. Bakal searched up and down the bank, trying to find an empty spot to set up their lines. Men stood so close together, their lines became tangled. Nets were thrown on top of nets until the river was a sea of twine.

"Koola mayoma!" yelled a large man with a jagged scar across his face.

"To-ana! He-lowmit uh fi!" the other man yelled back. He shoved the man hard in the chest, knocking him off balance.

The first man yelled more strange words and turned and hit him square in the face. In an instant, they were rolling on the

56

ground, arms swinging wildly. The men around them jumped out of the way, their nets and twine tangling into a heap.

"I think we better cross to the other side," Bakal said quietly. He led the way through the cluttered water, careful not to step through any of the nets floating on the water's surface. This was not an easy task. Makir frequently bumped against both nets and people as he gingerly made his way after his brothers. Each time he brushed against a net, he held his breath and prayed that these men would not attack him for his clumsiness.

The other side was not any better, but somehow they were able to find a small section of land that was not already occupied. Bakal laid his nets out in front of him, a grim look on his face.

"Come on Bakal, you know as well as I do there aren't any fish left in this river!" Haron said.

"Just fish!" Bakal roared.

He thrust a long stick at Haron. Haron grabbed the pole with a grunt. Makir grabbed a net and carefully walked to the water's edge. He kneeled down in the mud and plopped his net into the water. He couldn't move to either side without hitting someone next to him, so he just set the net in the water in front of him and waited. Not for fish. He knew there weren't any. He waited for Bakal to tell them they could go home. After perhaps half a day of empty nets, Bakal finally led them home. They walked back in silence, their heads turned to the ground in despair.

When they walked into the den, Tolah and Sharai looked at them with a brief glimmer of hope in their eyes. This glimmer was quickly replaced with dark, blank stares. Tolah stood and went to the door. He stared out at the empty street in silence.

Makir's stomach cramped as he thought of another night of roasted grain and watered down barley brew. This was all they had left, and soon this too would run out. His mother still had one vessel of grain kernels, but once that was gone, there was no hope of buying more. Hopefully the women had had more luck in their search for roots and berries, but he knew the valley was becoming as bare as the river. Every night his sisters came home with less in their baskets than they had gathered the day before. All the women of Babylon had gleaned every bush and tree, some even tearing the very bark from the branches. His mother had lost a great amount of weight and looked even sicklier than before. Makir was beginning to fear for her life. Just when Makir was about to give up all hope his father spoke the words they were all longing to hear.

"Many are leaving," Tolah said. He looked out towards his neighbors' dwellings. "The confusion and fighting is too much for them. Jaruah's family has already headed east, towards the great yellow river we hear talk of. Perhaps they think they can start fresh, build another city." A look of great sadness filled his eyes. "They will have to marry amongst one another if they are to survive, but man has done this before with much success. Only now things are beginning to change. Births along family lines seem to end in weakness and death."

He stared out the square opening in the wall and watched as men walk silently past one another. Some even moved to the other side of the dirt road, creating as much separation between themselves and their townsmen as possible.

"Yes, I have noticed," Sharai responded. "Perhaps these are also signs of the gods' anger. Perhaps we took too long on the temple? Oh, if we only knew! And now that there are no priests to talk to the gods for us, who else can help us?"

Makir's mother began to cry. His father went to her. He wrapped his arms around her and pressed her head against his chest.

"It will be all right, you will see," he said. "Perhaps the gods are fighting with one another. If this is so, we must wait it out. There is nothing more we can do."

"If only they didn't involve us!" she replied.

"It is as it is. Who are we to argue with the mighty gods?"

Makir listened to them with growing fear. When would they see? Couldn't they understand that these things they had worshiped were the very things causing them such trouble, not because they had any power, but because the God who had made them, the one true God, was angry with them for rejecting Him?

He silently pleaded with Yahweh, "Talk to them! Tell them, just like you spoke to me! Please!"

"I have. I am. They won't listen. They won't hear. They prefer the darkness to my Light," was Yahweh's response.

A shiver ran up his spine. Could this be true? Had God been trying to talk to his own parents the whole time? Were their hearts so hardened that they blocked out His voice on purpose?

Suddenly he remembered something Shem had told him many months ago, "All men know of God. He has given them this knowledge in their heart."

Makir looked at his family, each one different from the rest, each with a special gift they could bring. Siseral was serious and focused, always tending to the minor details, leaving nothing to chance. Bakal was strong and confident, ready to take the entire clan into battle, able to convince them all to give their very life for whatever cause he espoused. His sister, Seila, was sweet and shy and always knew just the right words to bring gladness to any heart and comfort to every soul. Even baby Mila displayed God's perfect design. Makir could see Yahweh's hand even on her. How could they not see His glory so clearly displayed in all He had made? How could they not see the very God who had formed them and sustained them?

Yes, many deliberately denied the Truth, but surely not his own parents! Yet, God had spoken to him, and there was nothing special about him. He was a mere boy, average and unimportant. If Yahweh had taken the time to speak to a ten-year-old boy, surely He had taken the time to speak to the head of an entire household and the mother that raised the children in that home. Oh, if only they would listen.

Chapter 8

Psalm 91:1-4 "He that dwelleth in the secret place of the Most High shall abide under the shadow of the Almighty. I will say of the Lord, He is my refuge and my fortress: my God, in Him will I trust. Surely He shall deliver thee from the snare of the fowler, and from the noisome pestilence. He shall cover thee with His feathers, and under His wings shalt thou trust: His Truth shall be thy shield and buckler."

"We leave tomorrow," Tolah said.

"But Tolah, where will we go? How will we survive on our own, without the help of others?" Sharai asked.

"How can we survive here? There is no business, no trade, no help from your neighbor," Tolah said. "I do not trust these people. Who knows what they will do, if they get desperate enough. No. We move. Tomorrow."

"But why so soon? Don't we need time to pack? What about Esthu and his household? We can't just leave them!"

Esthu was Makir's oldest brother. He lived on the other side of the village with his wife and three children.

"Esthu and his household will come with us. As for the rest the less we take the better," was Tolah's reply. "A few tools and some provisions for our journey is enough, the rest we will gather along the way."

"But what about food and shelter?" Sharai asked.

"We will find shelter as we go. We will gather herbs, berries and nuts along the way. It will be no different than what we have been doing here, only at least in the wilderness we will not have to fight a man for a few nuts and rotting berries!" Tolah said. "We will enjoy the bounty of the land! Your sons and I will hunt the beasts of the earth. When we get to a place that is good, we will rebuild our lives."

"But what about Haron?" Sharai asked. "He will be of marrying age soon, and you have already given your word to Gash. He is to marry Nila in less than two harvests." Sharai turned to her eldest daughter. "And what of Siseral? She too, must be wed soon and we have not even decided on a proper husband for her!"

Siseral would turn sixteen before the next new moon. This was the customary age for marriage, but as of yet, Makir's parents still had not decided who was to be her husband. It was not that they didn't have any offers, but instead, that they had had too many. Siseral was known for her studious, hard-working nature and gentle tongue. Everyone knew she would run her home well and would make a great wife for any man in Babylon. She also came with a very large dowry. The city potter, Elias, had offered his oldest son, but Tolah felt they could do better than a mere craftsman. These feelings only increased when he heard of all the new gods being added to the city. Each time Nimrod told of a new god, Tolah's business flourished and his social status increased. A lot of good that did him now. With Babylon falling apart and every man fending for himself, social status was as worthless as a temple stone.

"I will talk to Gash--" Tolah said.

Sharai cut him off.

"And what makes you think Gash will be able to understand you?" Her voice was beginning to rise.

"He will understand. I am sure he is thinking of the same thing. A man can talk with more than his words. I will go now." He left without another word.

Everyone was silent. This had to happen. They couldn't stay here. There was no reason for them to stay. It was a land of anger and confusion, of sorrow and fear. This was no longer their home.

The next morning they set out early. Nila was with them. According to Tolah, her father seemed relieved to see him and knew exactly what he was offering. Esthu had no problem with leaving, and came prepared with clan in toe. Everyone, besides the young children, carried a small pack filled with tools and other needed items. Tolah told them to make ready ten vases of water, dried meats, goat cheese and loaves of bread. Even though Makir begged and pleaded, they had to leave Filo behind. It would be too difficult to bring him. He would only slow them down.

Makir grabbed Filo's rope and gingerly tied it around his neck. Filo nibbled at Makir's cloak lovingly. "I can't keep you, Filo," Makir told him. "Father says you would be too hard to mind on our journey."

His eyes welled up with tears. He had tended this goat since he was young. This was his goat. Makir thought of the many hours he had spent chasing after Filo as the young goat galloped down the valley. He thought of all the times the goat had nibbled on his clothes, rubbing his nubby head against Makir's legs. Filo had been a faithful companion.

As Makir's family made ready their preparations for the trip, Makir led Filo down the desolate streets of Babylon. He would tie him to a post near the city center. Some family would be more than happy to have such a goat, old or not.

"You're going to be okay," Makir told him. Tears spilled down his cheeks. He rubbed his hand against Filo's short fur. "You will have a new owner, a young boy who will love you well."

Makir had reached the city center, the place where he had tied Filo the first day that construction had begun on the temple. There was one other goat tied to the post. Perhaps another family had left this one behind? Would this make it harder for Filo to find a friend? Makir's stomach felt ill. He wanted to hide Filo in his cloak and run far away.

"Yahweh, this is hard," he cried. "This hurts so much. Please take care of my Filo." He tied Filo to the post next to the other young goat. Filo pulled and strained on the rope, wanting to be free. It was as if he knew Makir were leaving for good. "I am sorry, Filo. Please forgive me," Makir said. He turned and walked slowly away. He felt as if his heart would break.

"As a father has compassion on his children, so I have compassion on those who love Me," Yahweh said.

Makir's heart still broke, but it helped knowing Yahweh was there, that He cared.

When Makir got back, everything was packed and his family stood ready at the door. No one said a word to him. Perhaps they understood his pain. Makir looked at the heap of provisions lying at their feet. It looked as if they had enough supplies to last them three new moons at the most. His mother insisted on bringing blankets, and Tolah allowed her. Who knew how long their travels would be. It could take many moons for them to find the materials to weave again.

In a way, Makir was relieved to be leaving. Perhaps away from all the confusion and distractions, perhaps now his parents would listen to Yahweh. What would happen now? Would Yahweh give up on his family, on him? No, He had promised. He had promised He would never leave him nor forsake him. Yahweh had told him this Himself. And Makir would believe Him. Makir chose to trust Him. Even if it took every ounce of his will to do so.

According to the slant of the shadows, they were headed northeast. The farther they got from the city, the rougher the terrain became. And yet they continued on. After a while, the days seemed to drift into one another, marked only by the rising and setting of the sun. The air seemed to get heavier and darker with each step. They were closer now to the fiery mountains, and although they all appeared to be silent, thick ash covered the sky like a heavy blanket.

After perhaps three new moons, the exhaustion was so intense Makir wondered if he could make it another step.

The sun was high in the sky when Tolah commanded they stop for their usual midday break. "Here we rest. We eat," Tolah said. They passed around a vase of water that had been heated by the day's sun. Makir gulped it greedily. "Stop! Save some for the rest of us, and for tomorrow. We do not know when we will find water again," Tolah snapped. His dull eyes scanned the bleak horizon.

"But can't we follow one of the great rivers?" Sharai asked.

They had passed a river hours ago, and although they had

stopped to fill their vases, it wouldn't be long before every drop of water was gone. And Makir knew there was no way Tolah would want to return, no matter how bleak and dry the land ahead. Sharai must have known this too, yet her voice still held hope.

"That is the way everyone takes. We must find our own path, our own land. We will not return."

Tolah rationed out dried meat and cheese. The portions were small, and Makir's hunger was great, but he knew the food must be conserved. Whenever possible, they gathered roots and berries along the way in an effort to stretch the food they had brought as long as they could, but they didn't always know which berries and roots were edible and which were harmful. If only the women had taken the time to learn these things from the old women in the city. At the time, Sharai thought it was more important her daughters learned the luxuries and social customs of Babylon that would help them marry a man of standing. Makir wondered if she now regretted this choice.

They continued in this way for many days, rising just as the sun was beginning to dawn, walking until it was high in the sky. They had found a few small streams along the way and had been able to refill their water vases twice so far, yet this was not enough. Their supplies were running frighteningly low. There was no way of knowing what the rest of their journey would bring. Man had not had much time since the great flood to explore and chart the land. Some said that Noah's sons had explored the land after the flood. There was talk of high mountain peaks and deep canyons, but where were these canyons of which they spoke? Did they hold water? Were their grasses lush and green? Were the mountains made of the heavy stones that could be melted into iron and brass?

At night Sharai laid the worn cloth out on the ground and

they all slept under the open stars. This was fine for such a clear, warm night, but where would they sleep on nights of rain? They all had been born in the city. They knew nothing of living off the land, of how to build shelter, of how to hunt. This was something they would learn together. But for now, they slept on the cool, soft ground.

Each day they set out as the sun was just beginning to rise over the horizon. Not until the sun was high in the sky did they stop to rest and eat. By now, they only had one vessel of water left. Tolah passed it around with a warning glare. Makir was so thirsty, he knew he could drain the vessel in one gulp, but Tolah had made it clear that they were each to have only have a few sips at each stop.

That day they had found a beehive hidden in some dry brush. It took much skill, and a little painful practice to scare the bees away, but they were able to gather a few plump honeycombs. The sugary syrup gave Makir's wobbly legs a quick burst of energy, but the sweetness made his throat parch. The sting of smoke in the air burned in his lungs and stung his eyes and only made his thirst all the greater.

When Tolah gave the signal to move on again, Makir feared his legs would not stand. He glanced at his young nieces and nephew. They didn't look well. If they didn't find water soon, they would all die in this barren land.

A sea of brown stretched endlessly before them. Each golden mound and sharp mountain peak they passed looked the same as the ones before. Every once in a while the endless brown would be broken by a lone tree. This small token of life only made the rest of the land seem more lifeless and desolate. As they wound their way along the base of the mountains, Makir began to fear that they would never find water again.

Luckily, they reached a small stream a little later. By the angle of the sun, perhaps three notches had passed. The adults ran to the water, the young children toddling frantically after them. As soon as they reached the water's edge, they got down on their hands and knees and drank directly from the brook. The adults used their hands as cups, gulping down handful after handful of water. The children plunged their small faces directly into the stream, lapping it up like dogs. Once they had had enough, the vases were filled. It was great to have a fresh supply of water, but the extra weight of the full vases would be difficult to bear.

Chapter 9

John 7:38 "He that believeth on Me, as the scripture hath said, out of his belly shall flow rivers of living water."

"We stay here tonight," Tolah said. "Esthu, you and your brothers find food." He handed each of them a lead spear. Luckily Tolah, a craftsman by trade, had purchased them years before. Sharai had teased him for this.

"What will you do with a spear, my dear husband?" she had asked. "Will you use it to scare a better wage out of your customers?"

"All men need spears of lead. A man must protect his home," Tolah had replied.

At the time, the purchase had been made in pride, but now they were all grateful Tolah had bought these tools.

Unfortunately, Makir and his brothers were not experienced hunters. They had been raised in a civilized community, where meat could be readily purchased at the city market. Now they must learn to live off the land. Not only that, but hunting in the wild was extremely dangerous. Makir was frightened. He knew giant lizards roamed the earth, ready to devour everything that came across their path. In Babylon, a team of the city's strongest and bravest men regularly patrolled for these lizards, keeping Babylon free from harm. But they were outside of Babylon now, far from the comfort and safety of the city. If they were to survive, they would have to learn to defend themselves.

It took all of Makir's courage to follow his brothers away from the safety of his family. And for what? After three hours of hunting, they came home with only two squirrels and a hare. The women had gone in search of roots and berries, but not knowing where to look, had not had much success themselves. For dinner that night, each person was given a few berries and a small section of meat, which Tolah had roasted over a small flickering fire made of dried brush. It was hard for Makir to sleep that night over the sound of his rumbling stomach.

They stayed at the stream for five new moons. The children needed time to regain their strength and the men needed to gather more food for the journey. For Makir it was a time of much needed rest. He even found time for fun. For the first time since they had left Babylon, he could play. He found a stick lying on the ground and talked his cousins into playing a game with it. At first they competed against one another to see who could throw the stick the farthest. This took great skill. The trick was in the angle of the stick, and if you added a slight spin to your throw, the stick could go even farther. When the older boys grew tired of this, they amused themselves by teasing Makir and his younger cousins. They tossed the stick back and forth to one another, always dangling it just above the heads of the younger boys and girls. The younger children spun around in circles chasing after the stick, their hands reaching as high as their stocky arms allowed. Makir didn't enjoy being the object of their amusement and so abandoned the game immediately. It wasn't long before his imagination took over.

In his mind, he was a mighty king, ruler of the land of the great lizards and flying beasts. He was clothed in a flowing robe made of the finest cloth, gold tassels hanging at his feet. His brothers were his loyal servants and obeyed his every command. They called him "Your Highness" and "Master". All the land belonged to him, as far as the eye could see, and beyond. Land that had yet to be explored, land he alone would explore and conquer.

In his land of conquest lay great riches, hidden under layer upon layer of flood laid sediment. He dreamt of entire civilizations buried under the silt and sand; great kingdoms with secret hidden tunnels and tombs filled with precious stones and the secrets of old. He alone would uncover the secrets of the flood. He alone would find the long lost treasures buried beneath the earth.

"Water! I see water!" Esthu cried.

At the sound of his brother's voice, Makir's mind focused once again on the events around him. He looked back towards camp. Esthu stood far off on the horizon, waving his arms frantically. As soon as he was sure the rest of the clan had seen him, he took off at a dead run. Makir's entire family ran after him, Esthu running northward so fast Makir worried they would lose sight of him. And he himself was already several paces behind. Makir sprinted to catch up, arriving only a few moments behind.

As he grew closer to the glitter of light, Makir's heart leaped for joy. This was more then a small stream. This was a large body of water, and where there was water, there would be food! Everyone began to laugh and cry simultaneously, their hope for survival renewed. Small green trees lined the shore. Birds sang in the branches. Makir ran into the water up to his waist. He thrust his face into the cool liquid and took a giant gulp.

"Bleeeeck!" He spit it out. It was salty.

He heard his family members gagging and spitting as well. Then silence. They all stood and stared at the clear blue water in front of them. Makir felt like he would cry.

"It is okay," Tolah said. "We still have water in our vases. We will drink that, but look at all the fowl. And fish. We will feast tonight. We will eat fowl and fish."

And they did. Makir ate so much he felt his stomach would burst. It was the best feeling he had had in a long time. That night he fell asleep quickly and slept so soundly he didn't awaken until the sun was beginning to pour its pink hues over the horizon.

The next day they gathered all their belongings and set out early. It seemed as though they had been walking forever. It had been many moons since they had left Babylon. The days were getting colder and the winds were picking up. The land became more and more raised. A huge tower of glistening white stood in front of them like a magical blockade. It seemed to reach the sky and was as wide as it was tall.

It was getting to be too cold to sleep under the stars, but there was no clay with which to build. Cold white specks covered the ground when they woke up each morning. When Makir tried to touch it, it turned to water in his hands. By now their clothes and tools were wearing thin. One of the spears had been left behind when the burden of carrying it became too great. Tolah said they could live with two, but the others had become so dull, they were not of much use. They would need to find a way to form their own tools and spears from the rocks they found scattered across the ground, but they spent so much time walking, who had the time to fashion tools?

Then one day, Makir's mother had had enough.

"Tolah, this cold is more than I can bear!" Sharai said. "And surely the children will not survive much longer. Can't you build us a shelter?" she asked.

"And where would you have me get the material for the bricks, and tell me, how would I bake them?" Tolah snapped. "The only stone I see is that huge white wall, but the minute I touch it with my hands, it begins to turn to water!" Tolah ran his hand through his gnarled hair. "We will find shelter in a cave. I have seen several mountain chambers along our journey. We will find such a place tonight."

There was a sigh of relief from all of them. Makir was so encouraged, he felt like he would weep. Living in a dark cave in the mountain wasn't his idea of luxury, but it sure beat waking up on frozen ground with numb feet and hands. Besides, then they would have time to make the tools they would need to survive.

"We will remain there until the sun burns hot again," Tolah said.

Makir wondered if the sun would ever burn hot again. The air was getting colder every day, and this was not just because it was winter. This winter was much colder, and darker, than any they had seen before. He had heard that the days grew colder the farther north you went, but he knew the cold they were feeling was more than that. This was a cold that no man had ever seen before, a cold that made your bones ache and skin burn. The sun was almost completely hidden by a layer of brownish-black smoke. And he had a feeling things were going to get even worse.

The animals seemed to sense something was wrong as well. Many were leaving. Many more were dying. The mighty Behemoths, with legs like bars of iron and metallic skin, at one time the king of all the giant lizards, were getting fewer and fewer in number. In fact most of the giant lizards were dying out. Food was scarce, the land was harsh, and the air was suffocating. Only the strongest animals could survive the harsh environment. Many animals moved south where the weather was better, but many more died, their bodies left frozen and stiff in the layer of white that covered the ground. Would this also be the fate for him and his family?

"Oh, Yahweh, are you there? Will you help?" Makir's heart cried out.

"Those who hope in the LORD are never disappointed,' came the reply.

"Here. We stay here," said Tolah. Tolah motioned to a dark whole in the nearby mountains.

The wind was picking up. The white specks carried in the wind burned their cheeks. Makir walked with his face to the ground to keep the sharp ice from scraping his eyes. Esthu's children began to cry. Their mother held them close, wrapping a thick but worn piece of wool around them and hurried into the dark cave. The rest of them followed.

Inside, everything was dark and damp. The air felt heavy and thick. They all huddled together near the mouth of the cave, waiting for Tolah to start a fire so they could have light. He spun a dry stick against the rock, faster and faster. After nearly an hour, a spark finally caught. Esthu was ready with pine cones. He held them next to Tolah's stick, close enough to catch the sparks.

Once a fire had been started, they all relaxed and began to spread out. Esthu and Haron gathered more wood and set it in the growing flame. Soon, they had a small but steady fire. The smoke filled the cave quickly and burned Makir's eyes and throat, but the warmth was worth the discomfort.

"Havilah!" The man Tolah had brought to be a husband for Siseral looked up and nodded. Tolah continued. "And Esthu and Bakal, we will hunt. Grab a sharp stick," Tolah said. "Haron, you and Makir make new spears. Use sticks, rocks, whatever you can find."

The four men went out into the howling winds to hunt an animal larger than ten men combined. This beast was a jumble of thick, coarse hair and had a trunk that swooped down to its feet. Large tusks curved from its mouth like great horns. These tusks ended in a perfect point and would make great spears. They called this animal the hairy long-trunk. A few of these giant creatures stood gnawing at the thin bark that covered the small number of trees throughout the land. With any luck, they would all eat well tonight.

Makir watched the flames dance along the caves walls. Smooth, circular stone daggers with pointed tips clung to the ceiling. Others, the color of goat's milk, pushed up from the ground. Swirls of yellow and cream weaved together in patterns of intertwining columns and indentations. Water dripped from the columns hanging from the ceiling to the ones pushing up from the ground, causing the towers to glisten like fine jewels.

Makir reached out and touched the cave's smooth, damp surface. It felt like finely blown glass covered in oil. The water was sticky in his hands. He looked around at the noodles of stone lining the ground with breathless awe. In some places, the rock hung out in thin shelves, as if carefully resting on top of an invisible stand. This was better than any hidden treasures he could have dreamt of! A slow moving stream ran through the center of the cave, winding out into the darkness. How far back did this cave go? The tunnels seemed to go on forever, their ends hidden in darkness. Drops of water fell softly from the thin cones hanging from the ceiling. The steady droplets created a musical melody that echoed off the glassy walls. There were numerous pools and puddles of all sizes, enclosed by smooth, round barriers of rock. These pools were filled with a water of the palest green, so pure and clear it looked as if it had been poured straight from heaven. As Makir stared at the beauty before him, his heart overflowed with praise.

"Oh, Yahweh, You are so good to me!" his heart cried out. "The beauty You have made is too much for me to bear! Thank You for bringing my family and me to safety. Thank You for showing me these hidden treasures."

His heart filled with a joy and peace that took his breath away. The presence of God was overwhelming, filling his very soul. The Spirit of the Lord had come to him, had filled him so completely, he had no need of anything else. Love seemed to burst through every inch of his body, a love so powerful he felt like dancing and shouting for joy.

Chapter 10

Romans 8:28 "And we know that all things work together for good to them that love God, to them who are called according to His purpose."

Makir looked across the cave to his mother. She sat propped against a far corner, baby Mila nestled in her arms. The light of the fire flickered on her face, framing her in a gentle glow. She hummed softly and rocked the baby side to side. Her voice was soft and gentle. The song she hummed was one she had sung to them all, a song of love.

> "The sweetness of a child
> Nestled in her mother's arms
> I will hold my baby close
> May she never fear of harm
> The night is quickly here
> The land has gone to sleep
> Oh, my child, you shall not fear
> In my arms you'll keep."

As she sang the song the second time, the other women joined in. Makir sat watching his mother with an aching heart. Was she still angry with him? Did she still blame him for all that had happened? Would her heart ever soften towards him again, or were they always to be separated by her anger and bitterness? Makir had not spoken to her since the day they had left Babylon. He had been too afraid to. But now, he was almost more afraid not to speak. He needed her love. He needed her reassurance. He needed his mother back.

Makir's legs felt weak and shaky when he stood up. What if she rejected him again? He didn't know if his heart could take that. "Oh, Yahweh, please help me. Please help me do this," he prayed.

Makir walked slowly over to his mother and sat beside her. He didn't say anything. He barely breathed. He stared at the ground in front of him, his heart racing. A sharp pain filled his throat as he fought back tears. Just when he thought his heart would break, he felt a soft hand on his. He looked up and met his mother's eyes with his own. They were shiny and wet. A single tear trickled down her cheek.

"Oh, my Makir," she said. "My sweet little Makir." She put her arm around him and pressed him close to her side.

Makir laid his head against her shoulder, hot tears pouring down his face. As his mother held him close, she began to sing once again. Makir closed his eyes and let the words of the song fill his heart and his head.

"Thank you, Yahweh," he prayed. "Thank you."

Outside the cave, a sound of cheers and laughter could be heard. The men had returned from their hunt, and from the sound of it, things had gone well. The women rose to their feet, their eyes expectant and hopeful.

Moments later, the men entered with a giant hairy long-trunk balanced across their shoulders. A large vein bulged on Tolah's forehead as he struggled to hold his share of the weight. Sharai clapped her hands when she saw them and the children squealed with delight! Not only would they have full bellies, but they would also have the thick hide to keep them warm. Tolah carried the carcass back outside the tent and placed it on the cold white ground. The women grabbed sharp stones and sticks and hurried after them. They got right to work stripping the hide and draining the blood. Siseral used one of the empty water vases to drain the blood into, and then took it about 800 strides from the cave. Here she poured it on the earth and covered the blood with the cold white powder that lay across the ground. They didn't want to attract any flesh-eating beasts to their cave.

Because of the white covering on the ground, the meat that was not eaten was easily stored outside underneath a large pile of stones and debris. Tolah worried this would attract animals, but they had no choice. If they brought it in, it would rot. So they hid it as best as they could, covered the area with strong smelling pine needles and hoped for the best. The bones were kept and set aside. These would be carefully shaped into tools and spear points. They would have much time to make needed spears and arrows while they waited for the earth to warm. Which was good. They had never made their own tools before, and it could take a while for them to learn this new skill.

Tolah kept track of the days by making lines on the cave wall with black ash. So far it had been 625 days, and still the cold remained. Because of the extreme cold outside, and the danger of beasts, they spent most of their time in the dark, damp cave. Makir's bones were beginning to ache. Tolah and Sharai were starting to hunch over, their backs rounded. To Makir, it looked like their bones could no longer hold them upright. The children's legs were bowing to the sides. It was clear all their bones were starting to soften. It was as if some sickness had befallen them.

Food was becoming increasingly difficult to find. The storms were growing more and more frequent, quickly killing much of the vegetation. The few berries they had been able to find before were now completely gone. Their diet consisted mainly of meat and more meat. Every once in awhile, his mother would tear some bark from the few remaining trees and boil this to make a stew, adding the needles of the tree to the broth. This seemed to ease some of the pain Makir felt in his legs and joints, but it was like chewing on a mouthful of twine. As the men continued to hunt the beasts with the long trunks, the cave became filled with the thick furs. These were made into thick coverings and sleeping mats.

The cave was beginning to look like a home. It was nothing like the home they had left, with mats woven of brightly colored cloth, and vases filled with olive oil and fresh figs, but it was a home just the same. Makir knew they would never return to the civilized land of Babylon, and so he tried to make the best of his new life. Still, he missed the comforts and pleasures of Babylon. He missed the feeling of the warm afternoon sun on your back, of soft river mud squished between your toes, of a warm gentle breeze on your skin. But most of all, he missed being able to run freely. The air outside was so cold he could barely stand to breathe it when he was still, let alone at a full run.

However, there was one thing he did enjoy about the cave. He had discovered great lengths of intertwining tunnels and secret passageways, many of them seeming to reach into the very bowels of the earth. His mother preferred for him to stay in the main cavern of the cave, afraid he would get lost or fall down some hidden hole, but he couldn't stay cooped up with everyone else all the time. He needed to explore! So, when she was busy with other things, that is just what he did. But he always took a lit torch with him and marked his way with ashes.

They had learned many things since their first night in this mountain. Esthu had discovered how to make colors from crushed stones. He used these to paint pictures of his hunting endeavors on the walls. Sometimes he would draw wonderful pictures to entertain the children as he retold their adventures and struggles on their journey to the ice.

The men had become expert hunters, and even though the animals were growing fewer in number every season, there was enough to provide their small clan with food. The women had developed great skill in making clothes and other items out of the hides and bones of each catch. The men had found smooth, glassy stones, which they shaped and sharpened to use as spears. In fact, they had replaced most of what they had lost on their journey or left behind in Babylon. But they had not replaced Filo. Makir's heart still ached when he thought about the frisky friend he had had to leave behind.

Makir spent a lot of time helping his mother. He also spent a lot of time with Esthu. He and Esthu were working to create new colors to add to their already growing collection. Already the cave was filled with many bright drawings. Esthu's children liked to watch them paint and Makir enjoyed making up stories to go with the drawings. Occasionally, when the rest of the clan were busy with other things, he would tell them of the great flood, and of Yahweh. He repeated the words Shem had told him, and added parts of his own.

Their favorite story was when he told them of the building of the great temple.

"Did Yahweh really talk to you, Makir?" little Ena asked.

"Yes, He did," Makir said softly. "And if you listen closely, He will talk to you, too."

At this their eyes would grow wide.

"But why? Why would He talk to us, Makir?" Malan asked.

"Because He loves you, that's why. He wants to be your friend."

They had asked him this question many times. Each time his answer was the same, and each time their reaction was the same. They would smile great big smiles and look dreamily out the cave door.

"They will listen," Makir thought happily. "When Yahweh talks, they will listen."

Chapter 11
Flood Stories From Around the World

Was there really a great flood that covered the entire world? Did all the nations of the world really come from a man named Noah and his family? Where did the different races come from? Are they products of evolutionary progress, or could they be the result of dominant gene traits expressed in different family groups? Were cave men primitive half-ape, half-man creatures, evolving from monkeys into humans, or were they intelligent humans who had been displaced at the Tower of Babel, struggling to live in the harsh environment resulting from Noah's Flood? Were their hunched figures evidence of their progression from knuckle walking apes to bipedal creatures, or were they hunched over from lack of vitamin D, vitamin C, and calcium, and the onset of bone disease?

If all mankind are descendants of Noah and his sons, then we would expect to find similar flood stories from civilizations around the world, and we do. In fact, there are over 500 different flood stories among civilizations from Australia to Greece, many very similar to the biblical account found in Genesis. It would seem logical then that there must have been a worldwide flood in which all people and creatures perished except those that were on an ark designed by the Creator of the world.

Obviously, I couldn't include all of these stories, but I did record a few for you to read for yourself. After you have read these, compare them with the biblical account. What parts of the stories are the same? What does the story say was the cause of the flood? How many survivors were there and why did they survive?

The Algonquian Flood Story

The Algonquian Indians of the Northwestern United States have a flood story nearly identical to the biblical account. In the following story, the exact wording has been adapted while special care was taken to keep the details intact. For the exact translation, see William Clemens' book, *Native American Folklore in Nineteenth Century Periodicals*.[1]

In the beginning, there was a great spirit. He was all-powerful. Nothing was impossible for him. Not only did he possess great power, but he also had the perfect wisdom to accompany his mighty strength. Everything in all creation was his, for he alone made the waters far and wide and the land that held them in. All life on earth, from the mighty beasts of the field, to the great fish in the sea, found their source in him. By his command the stars, moon and sun appeared and his hands directed their movements. Without him life could not exist.

At first, he created but one man. This man was the father of all men to this day, the great grandfather of all mankind. He did not want man to be alone; and so, he made a perfect companion for this man, a woman, the great grandmother to all.

---

1   "Native American Folklore in the Nineteenth Century Periodicals", William Clemens, Swallow Press, Athens, Ohio, 1986.

The man was happy with his wife, and all was at peace in the land. The two enjoyed the world the great spirit had made, and enjoyed the company of one another. But one day, this peace was shattered. One day, when the man and woman least expected it, the great black snake, the source of all evil, appeared to them. This snake was a liar and a deceiver. He created bad spirits that roamed throughout the land, demons to serve him in his quest for evil and domination. These demons tricked the sons of men and turned their hearts as black as stone. Soon, the men became as evil as the spirits the black snake had created, and there was great unhappiness for all.

Still, this was not enough for the great black snake. His aim was complete destruction and devastation. Once he had turned the hearts of man to evil, he sought to destroy their very life. To do this, he created great storms across the land. These storms caused much death and suffering. His storms were so great; soon water covered the entire land.

Above these waters were thick clouds. This is where the good spirit, the great spirit, sat, on top of the clouds above the waters.

Chinese Flood Story

The Chinese also tell a story of a great flood that destroyed all mankind save two, a young boy and his sister. In the following story, the exact wording has been adapted while special care was taken to keep the details intact. For the exact translation, see "Gourd Girl and Gourd Boy" found in *World Book, Chinese Myths and Legends*, by Philip Ardagh[2].

---

2   "World Book, Chinese Myths and Legends", Philip Ardagh, Chicago, World Book, 2001.

The men of China worked very hard for their daily meal as the filling of their stomachs depended on the fruit of the soil. Each day was spent in backbreaking labor, tilling the ground, bearing the sun, wind and rain every day, to grow only enough to last until the next season. With all of this unending toil, it is no wonder a farmer or two would lose their patience.

After months of rain and storms, a poor peasant farmer could hold his tongue no more. Certain the terrible weather was caused by the odious thunder god, he raised his fists to the sky in outrage.

"You hateful trouble-maker! You think you have the best of me? Ah! Come down and meet me face to face, if you dare!" Thus, forgetting that he was a mere mortal, the farmer made a direct challenge to the god of thunder.

The thunder god was enraged by the farmer's insolence. How could a small mortal man speak to the god of thunder in such a way? When the farmer told others of his intentions to challenge him, the thunder god lit up the sky with a loud, explosive bolt of lightning.

The farmer, made foolish by his rage, taunted the thunder god further and accused him of hiding in fear. Before the farmer could regret his words, the thunder god bolted down to earth, a large sledgehammer raised high. The farmer, proud beyond his merit, grabbed his trusty rake and braced himself for battle. Fortunately for the impertinent farmer, the thunder god was so consumed by his fury, he could not keep his mind clear enough to do any harm. The farmer, on the other hand, who was used to thinking quickly, stabbed the thunder god with one swipe and had him imprisoned in an iron cage before the thunder god even knew the fight had begun. Thinking that he had rid himself of all his problems, the farmer decided to make sport of his catch.

As a mortal, he should have realized the thunder god had more tricks to offer, but his pride was greater than his intellect. Wanting to tell all the men in the village of his great feat, he left his two children with the job of watching over his prisoner while he headed into town.

The children were delighted to be trusted with such a task, and promised their father that they would not give the thunder god anything to eat or drink while he was gone. Certain of his children's obedience, the farmer began the long journey down the well-trodden path to town.

The children sat silently on the ground, not quite knowing what to do with such a dynamic pet. Their curiosity soon grew to empathy and concern as they watched the god bake in the hot afternoon sun. He looked so meek and dismal. The thunder god saw the looks of concern on their faces and gave them the most pitiful look he could muster, hoping to invoke their pity.

"Would you please get me a glass of water? I fear I am going to faint I am so thirsty. I promise I will not do you any harm. I am a god of good repute. I always keep my promises." He made his voice crack as he spoke for added effect.

The little girl, always quick to acts of mercy, jumped to her feet, but her brother grabbed her arm and made her sit back down.

"We are not supposed to give you anything, " said the boy. "Father would be very angry if we did."

"Surely your father is not a cruel man," the thunder god responded. "I'm sure he didn't intend to kill me in this deadly heat. What good would I be to him then?"

The children looked at one another. The day had been much cooler when their father had left. Surely he would not be pleased if the thunder god were to die under their care, and it was indeed a very hot day. After talking it over amongst themselves, they agreed that one glass could do no harm. Easily excusing away their father's commands, they brought the thunder god an ice-cold glass of water.

The minute the thunder god saw the shimmer of the ice in the glass, his eyes sparkled. You see, he was the god of the storm, of the wind and the rain. Water fed his powers like nothing else; so that once he had had even a small portion, not even steel could bind his unconquerable strength.

The minute the water touched his tongue, he grew so large with strength and power, the bars of the cage burst into tiny fragments. Electricity snapped and crackled from every inch of his body. The children threw themselves on the ground, pleading for mercy.

The thunder god felt pity for the small children who had taken pity on him, and remembered the promise he had made.

"Don't be afraid, children. I told you I was a god of my word. I will do you no harm." He pulled a tooth from his mouth and tossed it on the ground as he rose into the sky. "I give you a new name today, Nu Wa and Fu Xi. Plant my tooth. The fruit it bears will be your aid."

The children stared at each other for a moment, then they stared at the tooth on the ground. The name the thunder god had given them meant gourd boy and gourd girl. What did it mean? And what did it have to do with a single yellowing tooth?

"Perhaps if we plant this tooth it will grow into great riches. Then father will not be so angry at what we have done when he sees how we have brought him prosperity in place of the thunder god," the little girl said.

Her brother could think of nothing else to do, and so agreed. The children quickly dug a hole and covered the tooth an inch deep in the hot soil. Within seconds, a tree shot into the sky, a fully ripened gourd the size of a bathtub hanging from its mammoth branches. So that was why he had called them gourd boy and gourd girl, for it looked as if they would be the keepers of the great gourd.

"But whatever shall we do with it?" the girl asked, staring at the colossal fruit above her.

Moments later the sky grew black with ominous storm clouds. The air lit up with giant bolts of lightning and the thunder shook the ground. Hot rain came down in torrents and by the time their father had returned, they were knee deep in mud and slush.

"Now look what you've done!" the farmer yelled at his children. "Because of your disobedience the thunder god is going to flood the entire earth and all life will be swept away in the raging waters. The blood of all the living will be on your hands!"

Even though it was the farmer who had angered the thunder god and the children who had pleased him, the children believed their father and felt great remorse. Tears poured down their cheeks as the water rose steadily higher.

Desperately trying to save himself, the farmer began to build a boat. Wanting a boat of great strength, he quickly melted down his garden tools and fashioned them into a vessel. When the boat was finished, he strapped himself in so that the rushing floodwaters wouldn't throw him overboard. Once he was securely fastened, he bid his children to come inside. And so they would have, had they not remembered the parting words of the thunder god, "The fruit it bears will be your aid."

"Hurry! Help me hollow out the gourd," the boy yelled.

The children climbed up the tree trunk, shinnied out to the gourd and rapidly began whacking at its tough outer skin. It didn't take them long to reach its soft fleshy center, and within minutes they had a nice, light, yet sturdy boat in which to ride out the flood. And not a moment too soon! For no sooner had their backs rested against the smooth, cool bottom than the flood waters pushed both boats over tree tops and mountain peaks until they rested at the gates of heaven.

Now, no human had ever traveled so far before, and when their boats clamored against the dazzling gates, the gods inside jumped in surprise.

"What in all heaven was that?" the lord of heaven asked.

"That is only man," answered the thunder god. "He trapped me and made a mockery of my powers, shaming all the immortals of heaven and threatening complete disorder and anarchy. I wanted to teach man a lesson he would never forget! I let loose my water and flooded the entire earth!"

The thunder god thought the lord of heaven would be pleased to hear this, knowing that he would be rid of all mankind and all the trouble he caused, but the lord of heaven was anything but pleased.

"Stop this now! Do you want to flood the very thrones of heaven as well! Take it all away! Now!" the lord of heaven bellowed.

Terrified that he had so angered the lord of heaven, the thunder god swallowed the waters instantly, sending both boats crashing to the mud covered earth. The iron boat landed with such impact, the farmer was burst to pieces, but the curve of the gourd broke the children's fall. When the gourd landed, it rolled steadily down the newly formed mountains, slowing as it went until it rested gently against a soft mound of dirt. When the children finally ventured out, they were amazed to see such bleak barrenness. They were the only two people left alive! They knew it would be their job to repopulate the earth, which they did once they were grown.

The Karinan Flood Story from Venezuela

The next story comes from the Karina people of Venezuela and was taken from Maria Elena Maggi's book, *The Great Canoe*.[3] Again, in the following story, the exact wording has been adapted while special care was taken to keep the details intact.

Kaputano was the god of creation. He watched mankind down below from his home in the sky and cared for them as a father cares for his children. One day, knowing danger lay ahead, he came to the land of the Karina people to warn them of a coming flood.

"A great flood will come soon, and the storms will be so great, no living creature will survive. The waters will surge through the rivers and lakes, overflowing their banks until they cover the entire land. You are my children, and I want to help you survive this great storm."

The people became indignant. "We don't know you! We have no father. We are our own masters. Why should we listen to you?" they said.

Yet, four men and their wives did listen. They believed Kaputano. "What would you like us to do?" they asked.

"Help me build a great canoe from the strong tree of the earth," was Kaputano's reply.

And even though there was not a cloud in the sky, the four men and their wives obeyed.

The boat Kaputano instructed them to build was so large it took them quite awhile to build, but once it was completed, they began to gather what they needed for the long ride. First, they gathered two of every living creature. Next, they gathered seeds of every variety and stored them in the center of the canoe where they

3   "The Great Canoe", Maria Elena Maggi, Toronto, Douglas and McIntyre, 2001

would remain dry and safe.

The other people still refused to listen, and continued to go about their lives as they always had, commenting on how pleasant the sunny days were.

Their laughs soon turned to worry as the sky grew black and thick drops of rain began to fall. It wasn't long before the rivers and lakes overflowed their banks, the raging water surging across the land. Higher and higher the waters rose, sweeping men, women and children up in its violent current. The only people to survive were the four men and their wives who were safely nestled in the canoe.

Although it seemed as if the rains would last forever, they did eventually cease. In time, the water drained from the land and the four men and their wives disembarked.

"What can I do to help you start your lives again in this land?" asked Kaputano.

The men looked out at the barren, mud-covered land and said, "How can we hunt and fish when there are no forests or fields for the animals to graze in?"

"And how can we build our homes when all the trees have been washed away?" asked the women.

Kaputano felt great pity for his children when he realized their land had been completely destroyed and decided the only way to make things better was to create a new world with trees, streams and creatures to fill them. This he did, and the people were very happy.

Ancient Greek Flood Story

The flood story the Ancient Greeks tell of is a tale of deceptive men, angry gods and total destruction. The following was found in the *D'Aulaires' Book of Greek Myths* by Ingri and Edgar Parin

D'Aulaire. [4]

Zeus was the king of all the gods that lived on Mount Olympus. All the other gods obeyed his commands, at least in appearances. However, the gods could be pretty mischievous, and often tried to trick Zeus into granting them their desires.

In the early days of the gods, a violent battle arose between them. All life on earth was destroyed, so Zeus gave Titan Prometheus and his brother, Epimetheus, the job of repopulating the Earth. Epimetheus was told to create all the creatures of the field, birds of the air and fish in the sea and Titan Prometheus was given the responsibility of creating man.

Epimetheus was so pleased with his newly granted responsibility that he started creating animals right away. As he created them, he chose wonderful gifts for each one. To the cheetah, he gave the gift of great speed. To the eagle, he gave eyes that could see for miles and miles. To the panther, he gave the gift of hearing. He had so much fun lavishing so many awesome gifts on all his creation, that by the time Titan Prometheus began creating man, there were hardly any gifts left.

Titan Prometheus felt very badly for the slow, cumbersome humans he had created and wanted to find some gift to give them to counteract their insufficiency. The only gift he could think of that would be of any worth to them was the gift of fire, but Zeus strictly forbid it. Titan couldn't understand why Zeus would deprive man in this way, so when Zeus was busy with something else, he snuck a bright flame from the fire in the temple on Mount Olympus and brought it carefully to earth. He didn't teach mankind how to produce fire on their own, but instead instructed them to keep the

_____

4   D'Aulaires' Book of Greek Myths, Ingri D'Aulaire, Bantam Doubleday Publishing Group, Garden City, NY, 1962

flame burning.

The men were so happy to have this gift, they began to use it to burn sacrifices to the gods of Mount Olympus. Zeus was enraged by Prometheus' direct disobedience, but was quickly appeased by the aroma of the roasting meat. Prometheus, on the other hand, was very displeased. He hated to see the humans waste the food they had worked so hard to raise, but he knew Zeus was very happy with the sacrifices, so he decided to help the humans trick Zeus. If he could convince Zeus into accepting the parts of the animal that were not useful to humans, then Zeus could still have his aroma without the humans losing any of their food.

In order to do this, he told the humans to take the bones and intestines of a bull and cover them with juicy, pure fat and lay this on one altar. On another altar, he told them to take the best meat from the same bull and cover this with tendons and bones. Once they had done this, Prometheus asked Zeus which offering he would prefer.

Without hesitation, Zeus chose the altar topped with the white fat, but as soon as the fat burned away, he realized he had been tricked. This made him so angry, he determined to get even with Prometheus and the deceptive humans Prometheus had created. This he did with a trick of his own.

Knowing that Epimetheus was ruled by his emotions and judged by appearances and not reason, he created a beautiful lady named Pandora and presented her to Epimetheus for marriage. This lady was dressed in the finest of clothes, given a voice as sweet as honey and a curiosity as urgent as a cat. Knowing that her curiosity would rule her sweet nature, he gave her a gift to take with her. This gift was a box fastened with a single hinge. Pandora was instructed not to open this box, under any circumstances.

Now, Zeus knew it would only be a matter of time before she

disobeyed his command, which is precisely what he was planning on. You see, in the box he had placed all sorts of mischievous spirits such as Greed, Envy, Malice and Hatred. His intentions were to cause humans enough discomfort to cause them to change their ways, only his plan didn't work out quite as well as he had hoped.

Pandora did open the box, just as Zeus had intended, and the spirits quickly escaped, all except one small spirit, Hope, which Zeus had placed at the bottom out of mercy. However, when the spirits started biting and stinging the people, instead of turning their hearts back to the gods of Mount Olympus, it only made them more evil and deceptive. The only thing Zeus knew to do now was to destroy them completely, all except for Deucalion, Prometheus' son, the only one on earth who was good.

Wanting to destroy the earth entirely so that earth could have a fresh start, Zeus sent a storm so great the entire land was flooded. All the living were swept away in the violent tempest, all except Deucalion and his pure and good wife Pyrrha.

When the storm had ended and the water had drained from the surface of the earth, Zeus looked out over the barren land and felt great pity for Deucalion and his wife. When they stepped out onto the mucky soil, Zeus told them to throw rocks over their shoulders. When they did, the rocks instantly sprouted into fully grown men and women and so the earth was repopulated once again.

● ●

God created a beautiful world free of death and sin. He made a man and woman to live in this world and have fellowship with Him, but man rebelled against God. Man's sin separated him from God and brought death and destruction to the earth. But God, in His great mercy and love, made a way to bring us back to Him. He sent His Son, Jesus Christ, to die on a cross to take man's punishment.

Because of Jesus Christ's death on the cross, all who believe in Him will be saved and reunited with God.

The Bible says that we all are sinners. Romans 3:23 says, "For all have sinned and fall short of the glory of God." Because God is so holy and perfect, He cannot be in the presence of sin, and therefore, our sin separates us from God. Romans 6:23 says, "For the wages of sin is death, but the gift of God is eternal life in Christ Jesus our Lord."

When we measure ourselves against other men, we may think we are pretty good. Surely we will get to heaven. We live pretty good lives. We don't cheat or steal. We have never murdered anyone. But God doesn't measure us by man's standards. He measures us by His standards, and to Him, all sin is sin. The Bible says in James 2:10 "For whosoever shall keep the whole law, and yet offend (or stumble) in one point, he is guilty of all." You see, God is holy and perfect, and cannot be in the presence of sin. In His Word, He commanded us to, "Be holy as I am Holy,"

So then we may say, "Surely if I do enough good deeds, say enough prayers, and go to the right church, then surely I will earn my way into heaven." But God says that our salvation has nothing to do with our works or good deeds. In fact, when we try to get to heaven on our own, we only offend God, as if we are saying, "I don't need you God. I can do this on my own." In Ephesians 2:8-9, God's Word tells us, "For by grace are ye saved through faith; and that is not of yourselves: it is the gift of God: not of works, lest any man should boast." In fact, in Galatians 5: 4 God's Word says, "You who are trying to be justified by law have been alienated from Christ; you have fallen away from grace."

God sent His only son to pay for our sin so that we wouldn't have to. He loves us and wants to be our best friend. All we have to do is admit that we are sinners, turn from our sins to follow after Him and love Him in return. In order to be saved, we must accept the free gift He has given us, eternal life.

If you have never accepted Jesus Christ as your Lord and Savior and would like to do so now, all you need to do is tell Him. Pray: "Holy Father, I know that I have sinned against You and I am sorry. I believe that Jesus Christ is Your Son and that He died to pay the penalty of my sins. Jesus, please forgive me of my sins and cleans me of all unrighteousness and help me to obey You. Come into my life and be my Savior. Amen."

Information taken from the following sources:

1. Dr. Parker, Gary. <u>Creation: Facts of Life.</u> Colorado Springs, CO: Master Books; 1994.

2. Dr. Morris, Henry. <u>The Defenders Study Bible.</u> Iowa Falls, IA: World Publishers, Inc.; 1995.

3. Lubenow, Martin. <u>Bones of Contention: A Creationist Assessment of Human Fossils.</u> Grand Rapids, MI: Baker Book House; 1992.

4. Dr. Chittick, Donald. <u>The Puzzle of Ancient Man: Advanced Technologies in Past Civilizations?</u> Newberg, OR: Creation Compass; 1998.

5. Dr. Whitcomb, John. <u>Babel.</u> Creation 24(3):31-33, June 2002.

6. Pierce, Larry. <u>In the Days of Peleg.</u> Creation 22(1):46-49, December 1999.

7. Oard, Michael. <u>Frozen in Time.</u> Green Forest, AR: Master Books; 2004.

8. Dr. Sarfati, Jonahan. <u>Biblical Chronologies.</u> TJ 17(3):14-18, December 2003.

9. Dolphin, Lambert. <u>Table of Nations.</u> <u>Http://www.dolphin.org/ntable.html</u> viewed 9/3/2005.

10. Clemens, William. <u>Native American Folklore in the Nineteenth Century Periodicals.</u> Athens, OH: Swallow Press; 1986.

11. Ardagh, Philip. <u>World Book, Chinese Myths and Legends.</u> Chicago, IL: World Book; 2001.

12. Marie Elena. <u>The Great Canoe.</u> Toronto, Douglas & McIntire; 2001.

13. D'Aulaire, Ingri. <u>D'Aulaires' Book of Greek Myths.</u> Garden City, NY: Bantaom Doubleday Publishing Group; 1962